THUG ALIBI

Makin' Love to the Law

KAY

Shan Presents, LLC

Thug Alibi

Copyright © 2018 by Kay

Published by Shan Presents
www.shanpresents.com

All rights reserved. No part of this book may be used or reproduced in any form or by any means electronic or mechanical, including photocopying, recording, or by information storage and retrieval system, without the written permission from the publisher and writer, except brief quotes used in reviews.

This is a work of fiction. Any references or similarities to actual events, real people, living or dead, or to the real locals intended to give the novel a sense of reality. Any similarity in other names, characters, places, and incidents are entirely coincidental.

Subscribe

Text Shan to 22828 to stay up to date with new releases, sneak peeks, contest, and more....

Want to be a part of Shan Presents?

To submit your manuscript to Shan Presents, please send the first three chapters and synopsis to submissions@shanpresents.com

Synopsis

Your arms are too short to box with Gahd...
Okera "Gahd" Ali is sexy, murderous, and yet, sophisticated, the only problem is, he's strapped with a plan of gaining more power and causing destruction along the way. He's taken aback and knocked off his square when he meets the equally sexy, Xiibria Sams.

Detective Xiibria "Bria" Sams is beautiful, alluring and smart. Without a man to keep her warm at night, deciding to focus all her time and energy into solving the brash string of murders piling up on her desk was top priority. Forgetting that all work and no play makes Bria a lonely girl.

Her partner and mentor, Detective Bryce Jones is just as focused when he isn't worried about Bria's absent love life or tiptoeing around case files in the precinct.

Bria's hunger for solving her cases is unrelenting until she's wooed by Okera's bedroom eyes, and gorgeous smile. The enticing crime boss/mogul is everything she never knew she wanted, but everything she needed. He takes his time with breaking Bria down while working to keep his nemesis, Carti at bay.

With a heart pumping pure blue blood, will the affection and attention from Okera be enough to sway Bria from upholding the law? Or will Okera be able to finesse his way out of a charge? Find out what happens in
Thug Alibi: Makin' Love to the Law

Chapter One

"Please, please!"

"So, you thought you could steal from me and I wouldn't find out? Nigga, I see all, and I know all. I'm Gahd, bitch!"

"Ga-Gahd, I swear, I'm sorry… I'll pay you back every dime. I swear to God—"

"I am God, what would my followers think if I allowed you to get away with stealing from me? You had one chance and you fucked it up, now deal with it," Gahd gritted as his men laid Ra-Ra's hand down on the table. Ra-Ra was still pleading for his life as he tried to figure out what was about to happen next.

"Gahd, please… I'm sorry, let me just make this right. Please!"

Ra-Ra's cries fell on deaf ears as Gahd walked over to the table behind him and snatched up the machete that sat freshly sharpened for the task at hand. Gahd usually didn't like getting his hands dirty, but when someone so close flipped on him, he had to make an example of them. He prided himself on studying punishments from the eastern countries and he had a special treat in mind for Ra-Ra.

While his men held Ra-Ra's hand out on the table, Gahd smiled as he assessed the machete. Without saying a word, he quickly turned around and brought the blade down at Ra-Ra's wrist taking his hand off. The large knife cut through his flesh like butter and blood sputtered from the fresh incision. Seeing him in pain brought joy to Gahd, and he was satisfied with his work.

"Aaaargh!" Ra-Ra let out a blood-curdling scream; spit hung from his bottom lip as his eyes bulged from his head in shock.

"Shut the fuck up!" One of Gahd's men said as he threw a right punch that knocked Ra-Ra out. He was laid out on the table, sleeping with the blood from his hand pooling around his head.

"What you want us to do with him, Gahd?" The man asked with a lifted brow.

"I can't do shit with a cripple... end that nigga and put him somewhere he can be found. His mama is a nice lady; at least she can give him a funeral," Gahd said nonchalantly as he cleaned his machete then tossed the bloody rag onto Ra-Ra's head. He walked out of the abandoned building behind Zeke, his right hand, and hopped into the blacked-out Cadillac Escalade. They pulled away from the curb and as quickly as Ra-Ra's hand came off, Zeke and Gahd were already on to something new.

"So, did you handle that other thing for me?" Gahd asked as he sparked the cigar that was twisted with some of the finest weed and rolled as big as a Cuban. He knew the streets were about to be on fire over the next couple of months, so he needed to get things in order early.

"Of course, I got you. We're hitting the club tonight?" Zeke asked as he grabbed the fat cigar from Gahd.

"Hell nah, I gotta go see what's going on with this crazy ass woman of mine. This lil' bitty bitch stays on some bullshit. If I didn't care so much about her, I'd drop her clown ass."

Zeke laughed and nodded his head before passing the weed back to Gahd. "So, definitely tomorrow?" Zeke asked jokingly, trying to get a rise out of Gahd.

"Yeah, we got business at the club tomorrow anyway. I'll get up with you later, my nigga," Gahd said before he dapped Zeke, watched him climb out of the truck and get into his car. Gahd's attitude and demeanor changed as his driver started towards the home he shared with Teva, his girlfriend of a year.

When he pulled up to his house, he clenched his jaw then blew out in a huff. His father taught him to never allow a woman to get too close, unless he was going to make her his wife. Gahd couldn't see past the end of the week with Teva, much less the rest of his life. She was always accusing him of fucking around and that shit could get tiring.

Reluctantly, he started up the driveway to the house. He passed the armed guards at the gate and continued up the walkway. The sound of music could be heard blaring from the back near the kitchen as he walked through the house. Gahd knew what that meant; Teva was cooking dinner and she was on a mission. When she wanted him to fund one of her expensive shopping sprees, she would cook a nice dinner and later, fuck like a porn star; she was predictable.

"Hey baby, I've been waiting on you all day… I made your favorites. Go ahead and take your shower," Teva said with a grin. Her eyes glistened as she stared into Gahd's eyes.

"What did I tell you about giving me commands?"

"Gahd d—" Teva started before she was quickly cut off.

"What did I tell you about calling me Gahd? You wanna play with me tonight?" Gahd gritted with his jaw clenched.

"Okera, I'm sorry… you know I be forgetting sometimes. I met you as Gahd, so it's hard to not call you that. O, I'd like to eat dinner and feed you dessert," Teva crooned with a sly grin. He hated when Teva called him by his street name. He wanted to keep that life and his personal life separate.

He laughed a bit before he started towards the bathroom. Teva had a way of making him laugh at her foolishness and no matter how much she got on his damn nerves, he couldn't deny how much he liked her. He turned on the shower and then shook his head as he stepped in.

"Crazy ass girl…"

Gahd came out the bathroom to Teva standing in a red sheer robe with a matching lingerie set underneath. Although she was slim, her curves were accentuated by the high cut underwear and heels she wore. He licked his lips as he watched her walk over and grab his hand, leading him to his seat at the head of the table.

∽

Detective Xiibria Sams ducked under the yellow tape and made her way to the cold body that sat in an old beat-up car. It was parked in the alleyway behind Rock of Ages Baptist Church. She cringed as her eyes landed on the wrist that was missing a hand. The victim looked no older than twenty-one… The sight of another young black man lying dead in the streets made her stomach turn. Visions of her brother laying face-down a couple blocks from her house kept her from hearing her partner call out to her.

"Xiibria! Cocky!" Detective Bryce Jones shouted repeatedly until Xiibria turned around. Cocky was the nickname she was given as a teenager because she was always beating the hell out of somebody. After her brother died, she was mad at the world and fighting was her outlet.

Bryce stared at her with wonder as he focused on the terror in her light brown eyes. She was beautiful and her dedication to solving murders drew him to her when they were first partnered up. A second-generation cop, Xiibria had that drive that normal rookies didn't have which was the reason Bryce took her under his wing. He taught her everything she needed to know about working homicide and closing cases. Had it not been for her father, he would have tried his chances with her.

"Damn B, I just had a flashback. This shit feels like I'm seeing Kareim all over again… Do we have any ID on him?" Xiibria asked, finally looking up at Bryce.

"Uh, yeah… Raheem "Ra-Ra" Smith, twenty-two years old; he has a small rap sheet. Possession, simple assault, nothing too serious. He must've really pissed someone off; they tortured him before they ended his life."

"This is some real life serial killer shit. Who takes a muthafucka's hand? Let's go ahead and canvas the area. That church has some cameras pointing over here, maybe they have something we can use," Xiibria replied before parting ways with Bryce.

Xiibria had a need to solve every case she was put on. To her, they were like Kareim's murder and she had to solve it. His case sat among the cold case files and every time she thought about it, it made her want to push harder. Xiibria made her way over to the church deacon that found Ra-Ra to ask him a few questions.

"Good morning sir, I'm Det. Xiibria Sams, Homicide. I just want to ask you a few questions while everything is fresh in your mind," she said as she pulled out her pen & pad.

"Yes ma'am, go on," the man replied.

"Prior to you coming out here to get into the church bus, did you hear anyone or anything back here in this alley?"

"No, it was quiet like it usually is at six in the morning. I'd come out here and get in the bus to pick up our older members. I take them to pick up prescriptions and food so that they don't have to get on the bus. I came out here and saw that car kinda facing the church blocking the entrance of the parking lot. I went over to tell the driver that they had to move and that's when I found him. I know him..." The man said as his voice trailed off and sadness replaced the politeness in his tone.

"You do?" Xiibria replied suspiciously, hoping that he knew something that could help her case.

"His mother is Sister Robin Smith. She's one of our choir members. Such a beautiful spirit, in church every Sunday and focused on living right by God. He's come to church with her a time or two, but he would never leave the streets alone. She cried and prayed that he would every Sunday and Wednesday at bible study, but he never did. It's sad," the man said as he shook his head and looked up to the sky.

"I'm sorry for your loss... I also wanted to ask you if you knew anything about the people he hung with or if Ms. Jones mentioned anybody wanting to hurt her son?"

"No, I don't know anything about the company he keeps, and she'd just say that she wanted him to leave that street life alone. I'm sorry I couldn't be more help." Xiibria turned around then looked at the cameras.

"Oh yeah, do these cameras work?"

"No ma'am, they just put them up yesterday and were coming back today to finish the installation. I can show you the appointment sheet from the company if you need to see it," the man replied wanting to ensure the camera install didn't sound suspicious.

"No sir, I believe you. Here's my card, if you find out anything or remember something else about this, please don't hesitate to give me a call," Xiibria said before she walked off. She felt like she was getting nowhere fast. She and Bryce met up near their car to go over any information received.

"So?"

"So far, there aren't any witnesses, we've basically just passed out cards… damn!" Bryce replied before he got into the car with Xiibria following suit.

"Let's head back to the station and get started on the paperwork. Hopefully, someone will call in with some info. I got a long weekend ahead of me and I can't wait to get it started; this week has really drained me. We've only gotten three of our now five cases solved, and I need a break," Xiibria admitted as she gazed out the window while Bryce drove, glancing at her every now and then.

"We'll get them done; just can't give up. I know how this takes a toll on you… Well, maybe this weekend you can get laid or something. When's the last time you had a man anyway?" Bryce teased as he stopped at the red light. Xiibria slapped his arm before laughing and putting him in his place.

"Don't worry about my bedroom. When's the last time you've been laid? The last time I checked, you were single too."

"I'm single because I have too much good dick to give to just one woman. And for your information, I got some last night. You need to let out some of that aggression… damn, Moses fucked you over that bad?" Bryce joked, but Xiibria was no longer playing.

Although it had been a year, hearing his name and having it thrown up in her face struck a nerve. She was ready to rip Bryce's head off and he knew it. Bria remained quiet for the rest of the ride and the moment they made it to the station, she hopped out of the car slamming the door behind her.

"Damn," Bryce said lowly, kicking himself for bringing up her ex. He trailed her into the building and over to his desk, watching her as she slapped folders on her desk with an attitude. He thought that she was sexy when she was mad.

Xiibria was built like a stallion; 5'7" with beautiful brown skin and 170 pounds of sexiness. Her mother was Samoan, and her father was Black, so she had an exotic look to her. She worked out so her body was toned with a fat ass. He always thought she should've been a model instead, but her hard work on their cases thwarted that idea. Xiibria looked through a few files on her desk before looking up at Bryce, catching him off-guard.

"That first case this week, he was found in a car too; you think they're connected?" Xiibria asked as if she wasn't just piping mad at Bryce.

"Damn, you're right... the other one was missing all of the fingers on his right-hand. The victim from today was missing the entire right hand. What does this mean?" Bryce questioned as he sat back in his chair with heavy thoughts furrowing his brow.

The phone on Xiibria's desk began to ring taking her focus from the files on her desk.

"Homicide, Det. Sams, how may I assist you?" She answered in a pleasant tone.

"I have some info on Ra-Ra's murder..."

"Good, you think you could meet us down at the sixth precinct?" She replied with hopeful eyes.

"Yeah, gimme twenty minutes," the caller replied before ending the call.

"Yes! This person may have some answers to bust this case wide open... I may be able to start my weekend off on a good note," Xiibria said aloud with a smile.

"I swear your ass is bipolar. One minute you're happy, the next you're ready to take everyone's head off," Bryce spat with a shake of his head.

Xiibria smiled and continued to sift through the papers on her desk looking for clues that she could have missed. A short time later, a short, fat Black woman walked through the double doors that led to their department with a look of worry and fear on her face. Xiibria hopped to her feet and rushed over to assist her.

"Hi, I'm Det. Sams, can I help you with something?"

"Yeah, we spoke on the phone about Raheim's case. Can we go somewhere private to talk?" The woman asked wanting to be out of the open.

"Sure, let's go in here. Would you like a pop, coffee or water?" Xiibria asked wanting to calm the woman's nerves.

"Yeah, sure. Sprite, please," the woman replied as she sat down. Her hands shook as she fidgeted with a loose piece of thread that dangled from one of the sleeves of her jacket. This was nothing new to Xiibria, witnesses feared for their lives the moment they walked through those doors and she felt like it was her job to comfort and protect them.

"Here you go. So, what would you like for me to know?" Xiibria asked as she sat down the Sprite can and prepared herself with pen and paper for the information she was about to receive.

"I saw the person that killed him... it was a light-skinned man with dreads. He looked pretty young, maybe twenty-five to thirty years old. I remembered him because I thought that he had a cute face and he was tall, about six feet. I don't know his name, but I remember his face. I saw a tattoo on his neck when he walked past me. He got out of that car, but I thought he was just parking it. I didn't know there was a body in there. I know that boy's mother... we went to school together. I remember when she found out she was pregnant with Raheim, we were juniors in high school. She was sixteen and always being a "miss goody two shoes," but Josh had something else in mind for her..."

"Ma'am, do you know of anyone that would want to hurt Raheim?"

"No, he was loved by everyone, so I can't see why anyone would want to do this to him."

"Okay, I want to thank you for coming down. If you remember

anything else, please give me a call," Xiibria said as she handed the woman her card.

The woman stood to her feet and started towards the door before turning around to say something else. "Is there a reward for the information I provided?"

"If your information brings in our suspect, I'll personally give you $200, okay?"

"Okay, good luck," she said as she hurried out of the room and out of the building. Xiibria walked over to Bryce to update him on what she knew, but before she could open her mouth, Lieutenant Dobbs pulled open his office door wearing a scowl.

"Sams, Jones, my office now!" Everyone in the room looked over at them before making faces like a bunch of kids watching their classmate being called to the principal's office.

"Yes sir?" Xiibria answered the moment she and Bryce were in the room with the door closed behind them.

"Do you two have any updates on that "missing finger" murder?"

"No, but we think they may be connected to the case we just picked up today. We're going to go back and interview the witnesses from that case and see if anyone saw the suspect we may have for the new case," Bryce said with certainty.

"Good, that's what I like to hear. I'll let you two get back to work," Dobbs said with a smile as he watched the two of them leave his office.

Dobbs was partners with Xiibria's father before he retired; he was also her Godfather. When he paired her with Bryce, he was hoping that his great work would rub off on her and it did. However, lately they were solving less cases together and it seemed as if Bria was doing all the work by herself. He was going to keep an eye on them; he had his suspicions, but he was going to keep them to himself for now.

"I'll go ahead and re-interview the witnesses from the first case. You can go ahead and get your three-day weekend started. I got this," Bryce said with a sly grin.

"Are you sure, you know you might need a real cop in there with you to get the job done," Xiibria joked. She hadn't forgotten about him bringing up her ex.

"Ha ha, you just work on getting laid and come back ready to work," Bryce rebutted with laughter. She rolled her eyes before grabbing her things and starting towards the door. As much as she hated to admit it, Bryce was right. It had been a year since she'd had sex. She couldn't bring herself to sleeping with another man after the heartbreak she endured.

Xiibria and Moses were in love. At least that's what she thought. They finished the police academy together and after being on the force for a year, they decided to pursue a relationship. He was always a perfect gentleman; gifts, trips, and amazing sex… Xiibria was ready for marriage and she thought Moses was too. That is until she walked in on him.

A year ago…

"Baby, baby, I'm home. Syria and I decided to cut our spa weekend short. I told her I was missing my man—" Xiibria started. As she walked up to their bedroom, moaning could be heard from the other side of the door and she lost it.

She pushed open the door to find some white bitch bouncing in her man's lap on the bed they'd shared for the past year. She just knew she was having a heart attack as she watched Moses stand by stoically, proud of the hurt he'd caused. The woman hurried to put on her shit, rushing towards the door. Bria turned and muffed the back of her head, making the woman fall to the floor. The woman jumped tough, but that was quickly shut down.

"Bitch, I'm a cop… I can kill you right here, right now and get away with it. Get the fuck out!" Xiibria gritted with a stone face, her eyes were trained on Moses. She couldn't let one tear drop. The last thing she wanted was for her or that bitch ass nigga to think she was weak. The woman climbed to her feet and ran out of the door.

"You didn't have to threaten her, chill out," Moses said calmly. It was clear that he wasn't moved by Bria's presence.

"So, you don't care that you've just been caught. Does this shit make you feel good about yourself?"

"Nah, I'm not proud, but when I tried to tell you that I wanted out you wouldn't listen, so now, you gotta deal with the consequences. You're a pretty girl; it won't be hard for you to find a new man," Moses said with a grin.

"You never said that. I would've cut your ass loose. I don't need you, nigga! How dare you make it seem as if I'm desperate. Muthafucka!" Xiibria shouted as she pounced on Moses, punching him in the face several times before hitting him over the head with the empty beer bottle that sat next to the bed.

Bria fucked him up so bad that he had to lie and say that he got into a bar fight and that he couldn't remember who the assailants were. The story was believed for a short time until everyone caught on to him and Xiibria no longer speaking. He had to work the desk for a couple weeks until his black eyes were healed, and his stitches were removed. It was the talk of the department for a month, but it was no laughing matter. She had to suffer in silence while continuing to work with him.

Xiibria shook her head as she pulled into the driveway of her three-bedroom house. She got pissed every time she thought about that day. She made her way into the house, kicking off her shoes near the door and then headed up to her bedroom. She flopped down on the bed then tossed her gun and badge on the nightstand next to her.

"Ugh, I need to run off this aggression," Xiibria said aloud. She stood up from the bed then went over to her dresser, pulling out a pair of workout pants with a sports bra. Lately, running and working out had been her only way of letting off steam. She got changed, put in her headphones and strapped her phone to her arm before running out of the house and down the street. She took in the sight of her neighborhood, looking at her neighbors retreating to their homes after a day of work with their children in tow. It was something she wanted for herself; she just had to find a man first.

After three miles of running, she was finally back home and stepping into the shower. She stood under the water allowing it to wash away the sweat that covered her body. After she took care of her hygiene, she stood in the mirror blow-drying her hair. She started to think about the cases they were working then hurried out to her bedroom. She pulled the notes from her briefcase and scattered them on her bed before she started to comb through the information.

"Is it the same suspect for both of my cases? What am I missing?"

Before she could dig deeper, her phone began to ring. She looked down at the number then smiled before answering.

"Hey boo!" She answered in a cheerful tone, setting her work aside.

"Hey, I hope you're not face deep in a ton of work. You're supposed to be taking a break from work this weekend," Syria, Xiibria's best friend said. Xiibria was always working and Syria wanted more for her friend.

"Well, all of us can't play at work all day. You do hair and makeup for a living while gossiping and talking shit, plus you own the shop. I, on the other hand, have to make this city a better place for you and your beauty queens," Xiibria joked while standing up from her bed and walking over to her vanity.

"Whatever, say what you want, but we're going out tonight and we're going to have fun. Now, go ahead and get ready, I'll be over there in an hour," Syria said before ending the call. Xiibria didn't even get a chance to turn Syria down. But honestly, she didn't know if she wanted to… it had been almost two months since she'd done anything besides work.

She pulled out her makeup case then started on her look, adding a simple but cute beat to her face. Once that was done, she walked into her closet and stood in the doorway, trying to figure out the move for the night. She didn't know where Syria was taking her, but knowing her best friend, it was going to be a club. Xiibria settled on a short, but tight gold dress.

She threw a few curls in her hair before she poured herself a glass of wine to prepare for the night. A smile crept on her face as she watched Syria pull up to her house. She couldn't lie, she was ready to cut up with her girl. It took only a few seconds for Syria to start blowing up her phone.

"What?!" Xiibria answered with attitude.

"Come on, let's go!" Syria shouted into the phone. Xiibria hurried out of the house and out to the car; she was ready.

Thug Alibi

"Wassup bro, I'm glad your bitch let you come out and chill with a nigga. No laying low for you tonight?" Koki joked with a grin.

"Man, stop playing... can't no bitch tell me what to do. Now, what's been going on up in here? I see the place is packed... you've been keeping these muthafuckas in their place?" Gahd replied with a stern look.

"Of course, this is me we're talking about. I told you that when I ran this club, this mufucka was going to bring you more money than you could count. How's that shit in the streets going... they find that lil' nigga Ra yet?" Koki asked with a scowl.

"Yeah, we're good."

"Aye wassup Gahd," Zeke said as he shook his hand. He was wearing a big ass grin, so Gahd knew he was up to something.

"Why you smiling so much?"

"I got that info on that shorty I was telling you about, and I talked my girl into getting her here. So, you better be on your shit tonight. I heard she's a little hard-up, some nigga did her dirty," Zeke said honestly.

"Cool. In the meantime, let's get some bottles over here and get this night started," Gahd said with his eyes scanning the club. He was always watching his surroundings, just in case some shit popped off. Koki waved over one of the bottle girls and told her to bring a few bottles and glasses out. The music pumped out songs that had the women shaking their asses and the men watching intently. Thirty minutes later Xiibria and Syria were entering the club grabbing the attention of every nigga they passed.

"Bingo!" Zeke said as he walked over to them, hugging Syria and introducing himself to Xiibria.

"Hey baby," Syria said with a big grin as she hugged Zeke.

"Wassup, I'm Zeke... Bria, right? I've heard a lot about you."

"Yeah, nice to meet you. I've heard a lot about you as well," Xiibria lied; it had been the first time she'd heard of Zeke. She had a few words for her best friend the moment they were alone.

"I don't want to spoil your "girl time," so I reserved a table in V.I.P for you two. Babe, I'll see you in a minute," Zeke said before he kissed Syria goodbye and rejoined Gahd and Koki.

Gahd's eyes were trained on Xiibria as he watched her standing next to Zeke. Her legs were toned and seemed to go on forever. She was thick as hell, her ass was fat, and her dress looked painted on. He could feel his dick jump in his pants as he watched her full lips form words that he could barely make out. He focused on her light brown eyes that shimmered under the lighting as thoughts of seeing her naked played with his mind. Gahd could tell from afar that she wore her real hair and it was long; he loved that shit. She was beautiful.

"Damn, it's so nice to finally meet your new boo!" Xiibria gritted with an eyeroll.

"I'm sorry, but I know how judgmental you can be. You're a cop, so anyone with the slightest amount of swag is a thug to you. That's my baby, and I was not about to let you ruin this for me. He's fine though, ain't he?" Syria asked as she stared at Zeke walking back to the table he shared with Gahd and his brother.

"Yeah, he is fine and so are those other two over there with him. But, I don't have time for that though. I need to focus on my job," Xiibria said making Syria roll her eyes.

"No bitch, what you need to be doing is finding one of these ballers in here and have you a good ol' fashioned one-night stand so you can loosen the fuck up. Ugh!" Syria grunted annoyed by Bria putting a damper on the night. Xiibria bit down on her bottom lip then glanced around the club; she did need a little TLC.

"Nigga... is that her?" Gahd questioned with his brow lifted.

"That's her, shorty is bad!" Zeke replied with a grin.

"She is... you better be careful with that big bro," Koki said as the bottles were brought out to them.

Gahd turned up his lip at the thought of him falling for her; he was too G for that shit. However, he couldn't deny how fine Xiibria was or that he could see himself banging her back out. He shook his head then turned around to turn up with his people; it was later for her. Right now, he was going to enjoy his night away from Teva's nagging ass.

"Cheers to new beginnings!" Gahd said as he eyed Xiibria then gulped down his drink.

The next day, it was business as usual. Gahd sat quietly at the head of the table. It was time for another meeting with his crew. The men started to pile in grabbing a seat where they could while speaking to one another.

"Alright, I needed to meet with y'all today to talk about what's going to happen moving forward. We handled the shit with Ra-Ra well and our witness has already made Carti's description a part of police investigation. My overall plan is to kill off anybody that can benefit this nigga, get him out of the way and then have my connect in the FED's off his ass after he watches my shine for a little bit," Gahd said sternly.

"Remember stay on point out here in these streets, but don't let that shit affect your hustle. We still need to get this money out here, so keep your grind as usual," Zeke added as he stood on the right side of Gahd.

The men all agreed and nodded their heads in unison at the command of their boss. Gahd looked around the room in search of someone, a confused look covered his face before he spoke.

"Where's Phil?"

"I don't know boss, we haven't seen or heard from him since early yesterday. I thought he was gone to handle something for you," one of the men said with honesty.

"Zeke, you haven't heard from that nigga either?" Phil was Gahd's other best friend and in command right after Zeke. Together, they were like three brothers who did everything together. It wasn't like him to not speak to Gahd or Zeke every day.

"Nah, I hit him up about ten times about the meeting and to hit up the club with us last night, but no reply."

Damn, where the fuck is he?

Chapter Two

The last day of Xiibria's three-day weekend rolled around and she was ready to go back to work. She had managed to get drunk, have a spa and salon day, and she still hadn't gotten laid. Being over it was an understatement. She chalked up the weekend as an unwind retreat and kept it moving. Syria had invited her over for dinner and she was starving.

"Hey boo! Come in," Syria said as she pulled open the door to her elaborate condo.

"When did you get new furniture and why?" Xiibria asked after hugging her friend and proceeding to the living room.

"Last week, I needed a change, plus I wanted to spruce things up for my baby when he came over. He didn't like that fake suede shit," Syria said with a giggle. Xiibria rolled her eyes and prepared to grill the fuck out of Syria on this new "boo" of hers.

"Yeah, about this new boo… who exactly is this guy?"

"Zeke is thirty, no kids, and he owns a few businesses. He's a good man and I've known him for years; we just finally decided to give this relationship thing a try. Once we all hang out, you'll see that he's smart, funny and cool to be around. Trust me, you'll like him," Syria explained with sheer happiness covering her.

Thug Alibi

"Uh-huh, we'll see," Xiibria replied cynically.

"Now, let's talk about you. We need to find you a man. I mean, bitch you're not even giving the toys I bought you a try. You could've at least taken them out of the wrapper to make me think you used them. How are you doing it?" Syria questioned with disgust. Going longer than a month without sex was out of the question for her, so over a year would be pure hell.

"I work a lot... I don't have time for sex or toys right now. And for your information, I'm doing just fine. I'm not trying to be out here fucking on any and everybody just because I'm single. I'm good," she replied. Xiibria knew deep down that she was only lying to herself because the look on Syria's face was evidence she could see right through her bullshit.

She was still trying to convince herself that she was fine, however, those lonely nights she rolled around in her king-sized bed were beginning to take a toll. Xiibria may not have used the toys, but her hand was getting a full workout on the regular. She needed some dick and bad.

"Whatever, keep fooling yourself. Let's go in here and eat," Syria said with a chuckle as she led the way to her kitchen. Xiibria shook her head as she followed behind her friend, hoping that conversation was over for the rest of the night.

The two of them sat down to fried chicken, greens, macaroni, cornbread, yams, and more. Syria had cooked a feast. She knew Bria would never cook like that for herself, so she did it for her. Syria worried about her, Bria would engulf herself with work and forget about the simple things. Love, fun and time without working were non-existent to her unless someone forced it on her. She was too young and too beautiful to be so hard on herself.

"I gotta tell you something," Syria said with a sly grin.

"Oh God, what?" Bria replied in an exasperated tone.

"My baby said he has a friend for you..."

"A what?"

"He has a friend for you and if he's anything like he described, I think you'll like him. You need to give this shit a try, even if you're just trying to get laid. A lil' dick ain't never hurt nobody... well, unless it's big," Syria joked. Bria erupted with laughter. Her friend was crazy as hell; that's why she loved her.

∽

Bryce sat at his desk staring a hole into the side of Xiibria's head. It was as if she was getting sexier each day and each day, it was getting harder to hide his feelings. He liked her more than he should have, and he wanted his chance. But, Bria wasn't one for bullshit. She didn't flirt, and she didn't take kindly to it either, at least not in front of him. He had a lot on his plate, but he wanted to add her to the menu.

"B, what the hell? Why are you staring at me like that, what's wrong?" Xiibria replied with a lifted brow.

"Oh shit, I was staring through you. I had a long night; I hung out with a few of my guys and we got fucked up. What about you, how was your three-day weekend?" He asked with a sly grin.

"I went out with my girl, had a spa day and just chilled at home."

"So, you didn't get laid?"

"Uh no, I wasn't trying to either. I was just enjoying my time away from work and you. That's a cute bracelet you have on, did one of your lil' girls make it for you?" She replied slyly.

"Now, you know I don't have any kids."

"Nah, I was referring to those young ass girls you fuck with... you made sure to card them?"

"You're real funny. For your information, she's twenty and she bought it for me. Why you worried about who I'm fucking anyway, you jealous?" Bryce said with a grin. The thought of Xiibria being pressed over him, made him feel good.

"Hell no, I'm just trying to keep you from wearing these, hot dick," Xiibria said as she held up her handcuffs while she and the other detectives nearby laughed. Bryce shook his head and returned to his work.

"But seriously, I also realized we're looking for the same suspect in these cases. The bodies were positioned in the same way and the trauma to the right hand before death feels like the same m.o.," Xiibria replied seriously.

"Yeah, you're right. We need to put a sketch out for more information on this suspect—" Bryce started before they were called out to another crime scene.

"Ugh, another day, another murder. Let's go," Xiibria said as they pulled up to the scene and climbed out of the car with Bryce in tow.

They ducked under the yellow tape that blocked off the front entrance of an abandoned building and proceeded inside. The body of a young man, riddled with bullet holes, laid on the floor near a pound of weed.

"Well, this looks like a drug deal gone wrong. I guess they took the money and left the product? That doesn't make sense," Xiibria said as she rubbed her chin.

"What's there to make sense of? This was clearly a drug deal. Maybe the people with this guy went after the suspect. Either way, this is one that we'll more than likely not be able to solve. You know these kinds of cases go unsolved. Nobody ever wants to cooperate when there's drugs involved," Bryce said nonchalantly. Xiibria didn't know what had gotten into him, but he had never treated a case this way.

"Say what you want, but I'm still going to bust my ass to solve this. Officer, do we have an ID on the victim?" Xiibria said sternly.

"Yes, the victim is twenty-nine-year-old, Phil Townsend. He didn't have any priors and seemed to be a straight edged guy according to the people in the neighborhood. He was a business owner and stayed out of the way. So, him being surrounded by drugs seems odd," the pretty young officer said as she continued to give report on what was learned about the victim.

"Thank you. Do you think these cases are connected?" Bryce asked causing Xiibria to frown up her face in disapproval.

"Hell no, this is something else. I believe someone murdered him and planted the drugs here to make it seem like a bad deal. The other cases were personal, this… this seems like a warning or a message. I need to dig deeper into this," Xiibria replied and walked out of the building. Bryce clenched his jaw and shook his head before joining his partner outside.

For the entire ride back to the station, Xiibria went on with different scenarios of what could have happened with each case. Her mind was like a well-oiled machine, it never stopped, and she would always work until the case was solved. Secretly, she was disappointed with Bryce's outlook on the last few cases and felt as if he was losing his edge. If he was going to continue to be her partner, he had to get his shit together. Xiibria wanted to retire with more solved cases under her belt than her father and that wasn't going to happen with Bryce bullshittin'.

The moment they made it back to the station Bryce rushed over to his desk and pulled out some files going through them without saying a word. Xiibria figured he was going to redeem himself after making that dumb ass comment about the cases being connected. Hell, a fool who watched enough episodes of *Law & Order* could see that there was nothing to tie the cases.

"Damn Sams, what'd you do to him? I've never seen him look so determined to do some work," Det. Tate joked, but Bryce wasn't paying any of them any attention; he was focused.

"Shit, your guess is as good as mine. I'm going to get some coffee, anybody want some?" Xiibria asked as she backed out of the room.

Bryce looked up once she was gone then pulled out a folder with witness statements. At the top, there was one naming Gahd as a suspect. As soon as he tried to slip the statement in the case file, Xiibria walked in and over to his desk.

"What are you doing B? You figure this shit out yet?"

"Huh, uh nah. I'm just trying to go over some witness statements, that's all. You come up with anything on those other cases?" Bryce replied nervously trying to change the subject.

"Nah, not yet," Xiibria lied. She wanted to keep the suspect she had in mind to herself until she was sure. Lately, Bryce had been turning down all of her ideas and the cases they did solve were because she went behind his back to work without him. She didn't know why he didn't trust her judgements, but she was determined to prove to him that she knew exactly what she was doing.

"Where's your coffee?" Bryce questioned.

"We're out, I'm going to go to Starbuck's and then head home. I can't sit in here all day. You know my best work is done when I'm at home. Anyway, the blue shirts did all of the footwork for us. You wanna join me, I'm buying?" Xiibria asked with a smile. Bryce smiled back then looked back down at the papers on his desk.

"Nah, I gotta finish this. You go ahead and enjoy yourself. I'll see you tomorrow."

"Alright, see you guys tomorrow. The sun is still out, I'm going to take advantage," Xiibria said before grabbing her jacket, the files and chucking up the deuces as she walked out of the office and then the precinct. They had been working non-stop for twelve hours and she was over it. She climbed into the midnight blue BMW her parents bought her when she graduated from the academy and peeled off.

She turned up the music, blasting YoungBoy. When she was off work she was no longer Xiibria, but Bria. She didn't care what anyone had to say; pretty girls like trap music, even if she was a cop. She rapped the words to *Solar Eclipse* with so much feeling, the driver next to her couldn't help but stare. The minute she realized she was being watched she started to laugh.

Shortly after, she was pulling up to Starbucks and hopping out with jeans that hugged her curves. The cropped jacket she wore exposed the holstered gun on her hip drawing attention to more than just her fat ass. Her long hair was pulled back into a ponytail, showing off her gorgeous features. Bria walked up to the counter and looked up at the menu for a second as if she was going to choose something different. Just as always, she ordered her favorite drink.

"Hi, can I get a grande coconut milk and caramel Frappuccino with whipped cream and caramel drizzle?" She asked politely with a smile.

"Sure, your order will be right up ma'am," the young man at the register said with a smile.

"Oh, you didn't take my money," Xiibria said as she held up $6.

"Officers get free regular coffees, but this one is on me," he said flirtatiously as he proceeded to take the next person's order. Bria smiled then put the money for her drink in the tip jar and continued to wait for her drink. She leaned against the counter and she watched as one of the sexiest men she'd ever seen walk up to the counter. He ordered a strawberry acai drink with extra fruit.

He was wearing a pair of grey slacks and black red bottom dress shoes. The lavender shirt he wore fit his muscular frame, but not too tight. His skin was smooth and chocolate while his eyes were warm brown and shimmered under the lighting with long eyelashes. He was fine as hell! Her eyes were glued to him as she watched his sexy full lips speak. He smiled and revealed perfect white teeth and dimples.

Bria could feel the wetness seep from her slit as she eye-fucked the shit out of the man. The moment he turned to catch her, the barista was handing over her drink. *Thank God*, she thought to herself as she hurried to grab her drink before finding a seat near the window. Bria giggled while shaking her head as she thought about the man at the counter. Her phone buzzed a couple times with a message from Lieutenant Dobbs interrupting her thoughts.

Dobbs: *I hope you have some info for me tomorrow, since you took off and left your partner.*

Bria: *Yes sir! We'll talk tomorrow. Goodnight Dobby!*

Dobbs: *Goodnight Bria.*

She had been calling him that since she was three years old and it stuck. She sat quietly panning through the files in between sips of her drink. The crazy serial cases she had, had come to mind, causing her to pull up the notes she had in her phone. The suspect that the witness gave her had a minor rap sheet. There was nothing violent in his background, but the description she got from the woman was dead on. She needed to find at least one more witness to corroborate the woman's story before she could even think about bringing him in.

Bria's face was contorted with heavy thoughts filling her mind. She pressed in a few notes on her phone and saved them to go over

Thug Alibi

later. Before she knew it, an hour had passed, her drink was gone and the sun was setting. She stood up from the table and stretched out her arms before walking over to the trash to dump the empty cup. She waved goodbye to the flirtatious barista then walked out to her car. Bria pulled open the door and stopped. There was a folded piece of paper on her window. She opened the note and read the words aloud.

"*You're too beautiful to look so mean... Whatever it is isn't worth taking that pretty smile from your face. Next time, coffee is on me. Have a good night, Ms. Officer.*"

Bria looked around to see if she could recognize any of the faces around her. Not one person in sight; she hunched her shoulders and smiled before she slid inside and started her car. The thought of her having a secret admirer flattered her and frightened her at the same time. It had been so long, Bria feared not knowing how to act around a man. It was hard for her not to be skeptical of every man she encountered. She shrugged off the idea altogether then turned up her music and took off.

Gahd leaned back on the lounge chair next to the large pool in his backyard. A thick cloud of smoke floated in the breeze as the strong smell of potent weed permeated the warm night air. He watched as Teva did laps in the pool that was blue lights. She climbed out of the pool and walked seductively over to Gahd. She was 5'6, but that was still tiny next to him. Teva was slim with a lil' bubble butt that gained enough attention. That and her pretty face were what attracted Gahd to her, but it was her personality once she was comfortable around him that, sometimes, made him want to run. She could be such a messy, jealous and vengeful bitch at times.

"Baby, can you get in with me, please?" Teva whined with a pout.

"Hold on! When I get done with my weed, I'll fuck with you. Chill out," he replied with irritation just as Zeke emerged from their house. The frown on his face disappeared when he spotted his best friend. Gahd stood up from his seat then shook up with his boy causing Teva to roll her eyes as she walked over to the bar behind them and poured herself a double shot of Apple Ciroc on the rocks.

"Wassup bro, I see y'all out here all booed up by the pool," Zeke teased knowing that most activities Gahd participated in was because Teva nagged him. He didn't like to do much more than make money and chill. Teva was younger and always wanted to do some shit or be in the spotlight. He gave Zeke a cold look before he sat down with him and began to speak.

"So… what's up with you? Why aren't you laid up under that sexy ass girl you got?" Gahd said. Teva sucked her teeth and made a face.

"Don't be hating cuz my bitch bad," he said addressing Teva's reaction.

"Anyway, you know my baby is a hardworking business woman. She's out making money, she doesn't have time to be laid up under me all day, blowing up my phone with bullshit and being out in the streets being messy. That's lil' girl shit," Zeke said aiming his comments at Teva. She held up her middle finger and gulped down the rest of her drink before sitting back and picking up her phone from the small table next to her. Gahd laughed at how true Zeke's comments were before he looked over at Teva and shook his head.

"Have you had time to go meet up with Bria's fine ass?" Zeke asked. Gahd smiled and thought about earlier that day. Seeing her with her badge and gun made her sexier for some reason. She was bad in more ways than more. He wasn't trying to rush his move, he was going to tease her a bit and then ease his way onto her. Knowing that she experienced a heartbreak was the reason why he was taking his time. Forcing himself on her would only cause her to pull away. He could tell by the way she watched him that she wanted him, but he wasn't going to play into her drooling and googly eyes.

"Nah, not yet. I'm waiting for the right time, but I'll let you know when I do." Teva's neck snapped at his response.

"Who the fuck is Bria and what the hell do you have to talk to her about?" Teva snapped as she stood over him with her finger waving around in his face.

Gahd stood up towering over her with murder in his eyes. He had never hit a woman, but Teva was going to be the first one he choked the shit out of. The look on his face scared her, however, she wasn't going to back down.

"You must've lost your fucking mind? Shorty don't ever in your life put your finger in my face like you birthed me. My own mama doesn't even play with me like that. Take your clown ass in the house!" Gahd roared and without saying a word, Teva did as she was told. She stomped into the house like a kid and Zeke was doubling over with laughter.

"Man, bro I thought you were about to whoop that lil' broad. Now that she's gone, we can talk business. The streets have been quiet; work is moving perfectly as usual..." Zeke started before his voice trailed off and sadness covered his face. His look alone made Gahd anxious and he didn't like that feeling; he needed to know what the fuck was up.

"Wassup Z?" Gahd questioned with a scowl.

"It's Phil... they found him in an abandoned house. Those muthafuckas had the nerve to throw a pound of weed next to him! Can you believe that shit? Our fuckin' brother was laid out there dead by himself and can't no nigga off that block tell me shit?!" Zeke shouted as his emotions started to get the best of him. They had lost a few men, but this one hurt... it hurt like a bitch.

"Damn man," Gahd replied as his voice began to crack. The two of them never cried, but for Phil they didn't give a fuck; they had to shed a tear. And together they didn't have to say a word, the tears they shed meant a nigga's mother was about to bury her son.

"We gotta get the muthafucka that pulled the trigger and niggas better hope like hell I find him or else I'm fucking the whole city up!" Gahd gritted with anger as his chest rose up and down with murderous heaves.

"You already know I'm on it, bro. Let's get that muthafucka!"

Chapter Three

"I still can't believe you took time out of your busy day to come meet me for lunch. I gotta pinch myself to make sure this is real," Syria said with a sly grin.

"Whatever, I needed a breather from that crazy ass partner of mine and work period. I've had a lot on my mind lately. It's like every case we've picked up, lately, has been reminding me of Kareim. Every time I think of him and his case I push myself past my limits. Dobbs has been on my ass all day about it, too. He said that I look like I'm losing sleep and like I haven't been taking care of myself… he sent my ass home for a few days. You know he's always my Godfather before he's my boss," Bria said with a shake of her head. She tried to argue Dobbs down, but he had the upper hand and she knew that she had to follow his command.

"Two extra-large, hard strawberry daquiris; here you go ladies. Your food will be out shortly," the waitress said as she sat down two big ass glasses with a smile then walked away. The ladies nodded with thanks before continuing with their conversation.

"Well, I'm glad I wasn't the only one seeing it. Bitch, you look like you've been missing meals and shit. You need to get all that together. Anyway, I needed a break from work as well… those messy ass hoes fussed and argued at the shop over some nigga. Girl, he came in to pay for one bitch's hair, while his other one was already there getting her hair done. It was a mess!" Syria fussed. Bria doubled over laughing at how exhausted Syria looked.

"They wore your lil' ass out, huh? I told you not to get in between those crazy hoes in that shop, let 'em fight. Wait, what the hell is a hard strawberry daquiri?"

"It's just a daquiri with a lot of alcohol, we can uber if we're unable to drive, chill out." Bria turned up her nose then took a sip before scrunching up her face from the strength of the alcohol. Syria snickered a bit before continuing.

"I did let them fight! I politely pushed their asses out my front door and watched in the window while they beat each other's ass and then his. It was crazy. But, I don't have time to let them stress me out. My baby and I have a mini bae-cation planned this weekend. We're going to fly down to New Orleans. I've always wanted to go. He got a reservation for a lil' house on the coast and if it's anything like the pictures, it's going to be beautiful. I can't wait..."

Syria went on and on about her weekend getaway with Bria smiling and throwing an "aww" in between sentences. She was enjoying hearing about someone doing something fun until her eyes wandered out the window. Although she was only able to see the side of him, it was a fine chocolate man dressed in a suit with a briefcase talking to a white businessman outside. He laughed, and his smile seemed so familiar. She was curious.

"Bria! Earth to Xiibria! Damn girl, I thought we agreed that there would be no police work for the rest of the day?" Syria fussed with her nose turned up. Bria laughed when she was finally able to break the gaze she had on the man outside. Syria was funny when she pouted like a lil' girl. She had a dimple in her left cheek and pink pouty lips that she was always flexing to get what she wanted. Her cute pixie cut showed off the length of her neck, making her look like a short, thick Halle Berry from *Boomerang* with hazel eyes.

"My bad girl, I just got so caught up in that fine ass man outside, whoo!" Bria said as she fanned herself and took a sip of her drink.

"Where? Where?" She shouted while turning to find the man, but he was gone.

"Damn, he was just—"

"Hey, I couldn't help noticing you drooling over here in the window, you alright?" The sexy man asked with concern, causing Bria to blush. She was shocked by how quickly he had eased up to her table and was using that sexy smile on her. Syria smiled while sitting back and watching the show, sipping on her daquiri as if it was tea.

"I'm good, I was simply enjoying the view. You just so happened to be in the way," she replied slyly. The man looked so familiar and she couldn't place him until he smiled and it caused her to melt. It was the same feeling she felt that day in Starbuck's; it was him.

"I'm glad you were. I'm Okera, it's nice to finally meet you," he said as he held out his hand with a smile.

"Xiibria, the feeling is mutual. You wouldn't have happened to see who left a note on my car that day, did you?"

"Yeah, that was me. And I would be a man of my word, but this isn't exactly a coffee shop and the two of you look as if you are enjoying those drinks a lot more than you would a latte," Okera said with a chuckle as he stood there in a navy-blue suit. One would never know how he took pleasure in putting his machete to the niggas that crossed him.

"Yeah, maybe another time," Bria said turning back to her drink. Syria kicked her foot under the table and gave a face. She wasn't about to let her pass up on a nigga that fine or possibly a good lay.

"So, if you give me your number, I can call you when I'm free for that coffee date," Okera said with a grin. His arrogance was smothering her, but that shit was a turn-on. He had a reason to be cocky; he was fine as fuck.

"Uh… I guess I can give you my number," Xiibria said as she pulled a piece of paper from her purse and wrote down her number. She handed it to Okera with seductive eyes and he couldn't help laughing at her. She didn't have to try hard; she was naturally sexy.

"Alright Xiibria, I'll give you a call when I'm free. Ladies have a good day," Okera said before walking out of the restaurant leaving the women in awe and Bria on the verge of chasing him.

"Damn, that nigga was fine. He looks so familiar, though. It's like I know him from somewhere," Syria said with heavy thought.

"Girl don't tell me you fucked him?"

"Hell no, I would remember a nigga that fine. But, you let me know how that works out for you. Bria bout to get some dick, Bria bout to get some dick," Syria sung with a giggle. Bria rolled her eyes then laughed.

∼

Gahd held up the piece of paper with Xiibria's number and smiled. It was something about her that made him want to risk his relationship with Teva. Her smile, her body and that sassy mouth, she had it all. Xiibria seemed to have her shit together, unlike Teva who was sitting around waiting for Gahd to put money in her hands every time he came home.

He slid the paper into his pocket and pulled the machete from his briefcase. There was business he needed to attend to before he could give Xiibria his full attention. After combing the streets, Zeke finally found the one responsible for Phil's death and he was about to feel the wrath of Gahd. The man sat tied to a chair with no emotions. He didn't plead or beg for his life, he was proud that he had done something to hurt Gahd.

"Neef, right?" Gahd questioned playfully.

"Yeah nigga, that's me," he replied nonchalantly awaiting Gahd's next move. Zeke eyed the man with shock; it was clear that him being captured by them didn't move him, so he wanted to find out just what would.

"You see this shit Z? This nigga got heart, I mean, ain't no hoe in this nigga," Gahd said with a grin, equally shocked at Neef's demeanor.

"Hell yeah. I don't think you can make him sweat Gahd. Gone head and let the nigga live… Shit, we might need to put him on our team. We could use a killer with no mind, right?" Zeke said in a sort of tongue in cheek tone.

Gahd walked behind Neef then placed the heavy blade on his right shoulder. Neef looked down to catch a glimpse of the blade and he still wasn't fazed. Gahd was growing tired of entertaining the muthafucka that took his boy out. He blew out in a huff before speaking.

"Let's see if this moves him…"

Gahd cocked back and swung the machete hitting Neef in the side of the neck, blood started to spurt out and in one more swing his head hit the floor. Suddenly, a smile replaced the puzzled looks on Zeke and Gahd's faces. They had finally turned that blank stare on Neef's face into a look of terror. Gahd straightened his posture before using Neef's shirt to clean his blade.

"Clean this shit up and make sure you dump this fucker somewhere his puss ass boss can find him. Zeke let's get out of here," Gahd commanded, wearing a mug that could put fear into even the toughest man.

The two exited the building and took off in the blacked-out Escalade. He needed to shower and prepare himself for his night at the club. The Garden was the first spot he and Zeke bought to mask their drug operations and it wound up being a success. An upscale night club in the downtown area, it was popular among young bosses and thirsty women. It also drew more attention than Gahd liked which was the reason he had his lil' brother Koki managing the place.

Koki was young and liked to be in the spotlight. His looks alone gained him plenty of women, but running the club made his pussy status go through the roof. At twenty-one, Koki was bringing in more money than any of his friends his age and niggas envied because of it. And just like Gahd, he had a murderous mean-streak, but he didn't give a fuck who knew. If he wanted to off a muthafucka, he'd do it in broad daylight to make a point.

The night was going to be about his new business venture. Gahd was partnering up with one of the biggest hotel chains in the U.S. and backing far away from the drug business. He wasn't completely letting it go, he simply wanted to be out of the limelight. He was just hoping his lil' brother was the right successor for his spot. Losing Phil hit too close to home and he was tired of the murder game. He needed a break.

An hour later Gahd walked in sporting black slacks and with a matching jacket. He wore a white fitted shirt underneath after deciding to keep it plain. He didn't want to do too much. As he walked through the club, it was just like every other night he attended, speaking to the niggas that looked up to him and smiling at bitches ready to throw pussy at him. Gahd nodded to his fans while his security made sure to keep them at bay. He spotted Koki and Zeke with a crowd of hoes around them, mooching off the open bottles of Ace scattered through their VIP section.

"Wassup bro, I didn't think you were going to make it," Koki said with a sly grin while shaking hands with the older version of him.

"You already know I couldn't miss this night if I wanted to. Can I ask you a question though?" He replied with a serious face as he looked around at the people close by them.

"Yeah bro, wassup?"

"Who the fuck are all these people? You know I don't like strangers being too close, plus Teva is probably hitting the spot tonight. Get them the fuck out of here," Gahd gritted. Koki nodded and dismissed the moochers from their box and returned with a grin. It was clear that he was high as hell, his red eyes were glazed over.

"Damn, you good fam?" Zeke asked eyeing his best friend trying to get a grasp of his mood.

"I'm good, I actually have some good news for you all and I want to toast up before everybody else starts piling in."

"Oh yeah, what's this news you have for us?"

"Y'all remember that big hotel deal? Well, those white boys saw something in me and they penned a contract with me. I'm going to have three locations built; Miami, Atlanta and L.A. Upscale shit with nothing but the best of everything. This shit is about to make me richer and get me out of this street shit. I'm too close to it and I need to back off. Zeke, I think you should join me on this and we can leave this shit to Koki," Gahd said seriously.

"Damn, so you're really serious about this shit, huh?" Zeke questioned as he thought about the proposition his partner had just brought to him.

"Hell yeah, we've had our run of this shit, let's move on. We've made millions and I think it's time to switch up our hustle. We can still manage the lil' nigga without being hands-on," Gahd said reassuring Zeke of the idea.

"That's wassup, I can't wait to be the new HNIC. Just let me know when you're ready and I'll step right in," Koki said, cheesing from ear to ear. Both Gahd and Zeke shot Koki a glare as if to tell him to shut the hell up. Koki threw up his hands then leaned back in his seat.

"That sounds all fine and dandy, but what about that bitch ass nigga Carti? We need to dead that war before we leave this nigga in charge," Zeke spat with a scowl.

"That shit is already in play, I'm not done until he's done, I told you that. I'm taking all of his land and once I do, he's done and I'm out."

Zeke nodded his head at Gahd then raised his glass.

"Let's toast up to making new moves and getting fucked up for our boy Phil. Rest in peace, my nigga." Gahd and Koki tapped glasses with him before they proceeded to throw back shots of Patron and glasses of Ace.

A short time later, they were joined by some of their guys and a few of the ladies that helped to create the empire Gahd and Zeke ran. Despite being surrounded by his people and getting lit, Gahd still had one thing on his mind… Xiibria. He had never been in love and he didn't believe in that love at first sight bullshit, but shorty had an effect on him.

"Hey baby," Teva crooned as she rubbed her hand across the back of his neck, interrupting the wild thoughts of Bria that plagued his mind.

"Sup shorty? What you doing with this lil' ass shit on?" Gahd questioned with a slight slur, he was starting to feel the liquor he was indulging in. Teva was wearing a tight black dress with a neckline that dropped to her belly button. Her legs were oiled with perfection and pedicured toes peeked through the red pumps she sported.

"You know I only dress like this when I'm out with you. Ain't nobody crazy enough to try it with Gahd," Teva said seductively while gazing into his eyes. He knew she was high, but he was about to punish her for it. She knew how much he hated women that smoked and whenever he wasn't around, she snuck and got high with her friends, pretending to be tipsy.

"You high?" Gahd questioned ignoring everything she said.

"No, I was drinking while I got ready, but that's it," Teva lied and he knew it. He nodded his head then grabbed her hand, pulling her into the back of the club.

"Where we going?" Teva questioned with confusion as she allowed Gahd to guide her into a dark office in the back. He pushed her over on the desk and hiked up her dress exposing her bare ass. He could tell she wasn't wearing panties; she was good for doing shit like that.

"Lay down," Gahd demanded while holding her down by the neck. His grip was firm and unrelenting. He freed himself from his pants and laid his thick nine inches on her ass, letting her know what was about to go down. Teva smiled in the dark, but the mirror in front of them allowed Gahd to see her teeth. She thought she was ready, but he was about to shut that shit down fast.

Gahd rubbed his swollen head in her wetness then pushed his way into Teva causing her to yelp out. She bit down on her bottom lip with pain-filled eyes while arching her back. That only made him want to dig deeper. Without warning, he slammed into her tightness, throwing an arch in his back with each stroke.

"OH GAHD!" Teva belted as she laid over the desk. Gahd used his other hand to keep a grip on her hips while still holding her down with the other hand.

"You do what the fuck you want, huh?" Gahd spat with venom.

"No baby, no. I'm sorry!" Teva yelped before her body convulsed with an orgasm.

"Yeah, you do. Don't ever do that shit again!" He added while pounding deeper.

"Oh Gahd, I won't!"

"Tell me... say that shit loud!" Gahd commanded.

"FORGIVE ME GAHD!" Teva belted. That shit drove him wild. The name gave him so much power and the praises that came along with it made him feel like a king. He pumped until he could feel his nut building then pulled out. Teva dropped to her knees as if it was her Gahd-given duty and sucked him dry.

"Shiit!" Gahd gritted with his head back as he shot his release down Teva's throat. She stood to her feet and wiped her mouth before walking out of the office and headed straight to the restroom. Gahd put his dick back in his pants before turning on the light and washing his hands in the restroom that was tucked in the office. He splashed water on his face in hopes of sobering up. He hated to be off his square when he was out in the streets; he needed to be ready at all times.

"What the fuck y'all go do?" Koki asked with a grin the moment Gahd and Teva returned.

"Damn, you're nosy!" Teva spat before grabbing the bottle of Ace and drinking out of it.

"Aye don't drink out that bottle, she's been back there sucking dick," Koki said seriously causing the whole section to erupt with laughter. Gahd shook his head then grabbed Teva's face when she was about to say something. He knew her mouth could be vicious, and he didn't feel like getting between her and his brother. She looked at him then took a swig of the Ace. *This nigga!*

∽

Bryce sat in the unmarked car, waiting under the viaduct in the dark. He was meeting up with his C.I (informant). He needed to get some information on the murders that had been happening and who was behind them. Boo was a former thug turned snitch and was staying way under the radar. He seemed to be around the right people at the right time and had a way of getting the

Thug Alibi

information Bria and Bryce needed for their gang-related homicides.

"Damn man, I told you not to ride in the same car as last time. You gon' get a nigga caught up on some bullshit. Where's my fucking money?" Boo said nervously while looking around.

"Here snitch!" Bryce spat as he tossed five bills in Boo's face. He hated having to pay for information he could beat out of someone for free, but for the sake of his badge he was going to get it the right way, this time.

"Fuck you, pig! Now, listen up... You need to go out there and find that nigga Brisco. He has intel on whatever it is that motivated Gahd to start up this lil' tit for tat war between him and Carti. But, I'm gon' tell you right now, this nigga ain't no walk in the park. He'd give his life for Gahd and going against him is an unthinkable act to him, so I don't know how you're going to break this young nigga," Boo said just loud enough for Bryce to take in everything he told him. His eyes were still shifting between every window on the car as he watched his surroundings.

"Where can I find this Brisco?"

"He's usually around the Ave., probably trying to holla at some hoes. Around this time of night, he's going back to the spot to stash the money he's collected from his workers. There's a safe in there, but it's all kinds of cameras and shit, sending live footage. Can you believe this nigga Gahd, has mufuckas clocking in and out, legally? They watch his drug spots and report strange behavior to him," Boo confessed. He was singing like a bird and his only hope was that Gahd never found out.

"Damn, he really thinks he's God, huh? So how am I supposed to get him alone to question him?" Bryce replied with a lifted brow.

"Your best bet is to wait for him to come out; he'll park behind that garage. He's always alone with his lil' pistol. Most muthafuckas are too scared to step that far into Gahd's territory to try anything, so these niggas are comfortable. Move in on him then and snatch him up but be quick."

"Why does it feel like you're sending me in to do a job? I'm a cop, I just want to question him, that's it," Bryce replied slyly.

Boo wasn't a fool; he knew exactly what Bryce was and just a cop wasn't it. It was no surprise that the people he sent Bryce to would somehow end up dead. Either he was killing them or sending someone else to do his dirty work.

"Whatever, I'm out," Boo replied as he tossed a small piece of paper with an address to Bryce and hurried out the car before disappearing into the darkness. Bryce took a deep breath then took off towards the Ave.

∽

"Baby, I don't like that you didn't defend me tonight. Your brother says whatever he wants to me and I have to sit there and take it," Teva fussed with a roll of her eyes as she stepped out of the shower. Gahd knew it coming, but he really wasn't in the mood to go back and forth with her over bullshit.

"Look, it's not that I'm letting him say whatever, but I know how you two are. If I didn't intervene, both of you would've been ready to box it out. I can't have my woman and brother fighting and definitely not in my spot; that's where I make my money. You two can bicker here at the house anytime," Gahd said with a shake of his head. He stepped into his boxer briefs and stood in front of the mirror drying up the rest of the water on his muscular chest.

Teva stood behind him staring at the tattoo of a muscular, God-like man sitting on a throne. It covered the top of Gahd's back and made his toned body look even more intimidating. She was in love with everything about him, but some his ways made him seem impossible. They'd been together for a little over a year and she still felt as if she was fighting to prove her love for him.

They met on one of his blocks as she bounced down the street with her friend. It was their regular routine; get fly as hell and strut their shit until one of the ballers scooped them up. Gahd called her over and she'd been his bitch ever since. She knew the real reason he hollered at her and not her thick ass friend, but she didn't care. Teva took advantage of the situation and had been milking it since. But, she was starting to notice a change in him. Gahd was pulling away from that street shit and starting to be more about his business. She hated a lame ass nigga; a thug was what she needed in her life.

"I hear you, but next time can you at least let me defend myself? I felt like such a fool, just sitting there with my mouth shut tight as all your friends laughed at my expense."

"Yeah, you just make sure you keep it classy in these streets. I don't need a ghetto bitch fighting and running her mouth hanging on my arm. I'm a boss, a businessman and I need my woman to be just as reserved as me," Gahd commanded with his face becoming more serious.

"I got it babe. Oh yeah, I wanted to tell you the good news earlier... I enrolled in school and I'll be starting towards my bachelor's degree in the fall," Teva said proudly with a smile.

"That's good, baby. I'm proud of you... now, you'll be able to make your own money and leave mines alone," Gahd said before walking out of the bathroom, leaving Teva in awe.

"Thanks," Teva said lowly with a sad look on her face.

I'll never be good enough.

Chapter Four

*I*t had been almost a week since he'd gotten Xiibria's number, but he needed to be able to give her his full attention. She wasn't just some thot he could flash money in front of and she'd come running. He had to actually strap on his charm to please her.

Okera held up the number then pressed it into his phone before pressing send.

"Hello?" She answered after three rings.

"Hi, this isn't a bad time is it?" Okera replied cautiously.

"It depends, who is this?"

"You give your number out to that many people?" He was being sly, and it brought a smile to her face. Xiibria rolled her eyes and immediately she knew it was him.

"Nah, just this one guy. I think he's a stalker, but I can handle him," she said playfully.

"Oh, I'm a stalker now? How have you been Ms. Xiibria?" Okera said getting to the reason for his call.

"I've been well… working hard as usual. How about you?"

"The same. I was thinking about you and I wanted to know if I could take you out for dinner tonight?" Okera didn't want to push, but at the same time, he was ready for them to get to know one another just enough for him to make his next move. Nah, he wasn't just trying to fuck, he wanted to make her his.

"Hmm... I am free tonight and I could use a good, expensive meal... Alright, it's a date," Xiibria said with more excitement than she'd like. She slapped her hand on her forehead, hoping she didn't sound too thirsty. The truth was, she had been thinking about Okera a lot and was secretly hoping he'd call one day.

"Good, I can have my driver pick you up at 7—" He started before she cut him off.

"I think I'll meet you there, text me the address and I'll see you at 7 sharp," Xiibria replied bluntly. She was working on coming off less abrasive. It had been so long since she'd been intimate, she felt like she'd lost her finesse.

"Okay ma'am, whatever you say," Okera said taking heed of her tone and ending the call.

"Damn, I hope I didn't ruin it. Oh shit, what am I going to wear?" She yelled as she ran over to her closet. Bria was fresh out of the shower and running around the room with her hair wet. The FEDs were barging their way into the cases she and Bryce had, and her murder cases were about to turn into a R.I.C.O. They were allowing the two of them to still work the homicides to build up a case on a suspect. She didn't understand why they were involved when all she had was a description and no name.

"This is perfect!" Bria exclaimed as she held up a silver dress that stopped at the knees. The neckline was adorned with crystals and cut down just below her breasts. It was a Dior dress she bought when she was having retail therapy, compliments of Moses' credit cards. She had managed to spend $10k in less than five hours and it still didn't feel good.

The tag still dangled on the dress revealing the $1500 price she paid for it. She laid it on her bed and looked around in her closet for shoes to match.

"A silver dress needs silver shoes. Yup, this is it," she said as she picked up the silver heels. It was a perfect match. She rushed over to her vanity then stared at her hair in the mirror, it was her next battle.

"Shit! His ass better be taking me somewhere nice," Bria gritted as she grabbed the blow dryer and started on her head.

An hour later, her hair was straightened and adorned curls that fit perfectly with the dress. She couldn't get out of the mirror; her makeup was flawless and so was her hair. Bria rushed over to her phone and propped up her camera to take a picture, she needed to remember this moment. It might've been the last time she dressed up for a date.

"Damn, I look good. I'm a bad bitch, I'm a bad bitch!" She recited in the mirror before she caught a glimpse of the time; it was 6:15 and she needed to go. Bria hurried to grab a jacket and her clutch before making a mad dash out to her car.

After punching the address in the GPS, she smiled. He was taking her to Parle', an expensive restaurant downtown that was popular for having the best comfort food. Bria was thanking God that she wasn't overdressed for the night. She'd never been there but heard about the strict bougie dress code. The closer she got to the restaurant, the more nervous she got. It hadn't hit her at first, but she was going on a date despite her rants of "never getting caught up with another nigga again." All Bria could think about was her letting Syria talk her into it, and how she was going to kill her if it went bad.

Bria made it to the restaurant and got valet parking with five minutes to spare. As she stood in front of the restaurant, she stared at the name above the door. She had to see this through; being a quitter just wasn't her. She adjusted her dress and took a deep breath before walking in and up to the hostess.

"Hi, I'm meeting someone here; Okera," she said remembering that she didn't have a last name for him.

"Oh yes, he's been expecting you," the short girl said. Her long hair framed her pretty face and gave her an innocent look. Her eyes were mysterious as she eyed Bria then smiled and nodded at her appearance. *I guess she approves*, Bria thought to herself as she followed the cute hostess back to a private section where Okera was waiting. He stood next to her chair with a look that gave her butterflies. He was so damn sexy.

"I'm glad you could make it... I see you're serious about your punctuality, I like that. Have a seat beautiful," Okera said with a lick of his lips as he watched Bria slide into the chair, her fat ass hypnotized him and suddenly he was stuck holding the chair instead of pushing it.

"Uh, I got it. I guess I'm too heavy to push, huh?" She asked as she pulled her seat up to the table.

"Oh no, I—let's have a drink."

Bria's eyes sized Okera up from head to toe. His hair was freshly cut, and his waves were making her seasick. The tattoos on his chest fought to remain hidden under the black buttoned shirt. The top three buttons were undone, allowing the scent of his cologne to flow across the table and pass the fresh flowers. She figured his scent was exactly what a million bucks would smell like... amazing. The sleeves of his shirt fit snug over his muscular arms and she could only imagine how he would look naked.

"Wine?" The waiter said as he walked over with a cart holding a bucket of expensive wine on rocks. Bria nodded and held up her glass with her eyes fixed on Okera.

"You look— damn, you look good. I can't lie, I knew you were beautiful, but to see you dressed like this... I can spend every weekend with you, a fancy dinner and this look," Okera said catching himself before he started to sound thirsty. He was a G, but he couldn't help his attraction to Xiibria.

She blushed before she spoke; it had been a long time since a man of his caliber spoke those words to her. I mean, she had her share of thugs, broke men and criminals telling her how sexy and thick she was, but to hear it from him meant something. Bria took a sip of her wine and played it cool.

"Thanks, you don't look to shabby yourself. This place is awesome, the view is so beautiful, wow! Thank you again for inviting me. So, let's talk and get to know one another," Bria said smoothly with a glimmer in her eyes. She had Okera's full attention and he was hoping she didn't let up.

"Sure, I'll tell you a little about myself. My name is Okera Ali and I'm a thirty-year-old business owner. I own a couple clubs, two restaurants, including this one, and I just bought into the hotel business; Hilton. I'm single with no children, what about you?" Okera said as he picked up his glass and took a sip.

"You own this place, I've heard so many good things about it. Congrats on your success and your new endeavors. Well, I'm Xiibria Sams, I'm twenty-eight and I work for the city. I'm a court officer," Bria lied. She hated to tell men she was a homicide detective, they were always judging her and acting as if she couldn't hold her own.

"Okay, that's why you had that gun that day, I thought you were a police officer. Are you single miss Xiibria?"

"Yes, very single and I have been for quite some time now. Why are you single?" Bria asked curiously.

"I'm looking for the right woman; I date, but I haven't found her yet," Okera said thinking about Teva, probably at home or out spending his money with no regard for the grind he put into getting what he had.

"I feel you on that, but sometimes, men ain't shit! They lie, cheat, steal... they're like criminals of love. Ugh!" Bria grunted as she thought about Moses fucking over her.

"Damn, I see some nigga has broken your heart in the past. You have to leave the past where it is and move forward. He wasn't meant for you, so he was removed from your life, consider yourself lucky. You could've married him," Okera said slyly before his eyes cut over to the waiter bringing out their salads.

She thought about what he said as she quietly stuck a forkful of salad into her mouth. She was so sure marriage was the next step for her and Moses that she looked over all the clues that were right in front of her. Okera quietly ate his salad as if he was allowing her to process the polite read he'd just given her. Bria looked up to catch his glance and smiled before she began to speak.

"What kind of woman are you looking for?"

"Smart, loyal, beautiful, classy and hard-working; I don't ask for much, just the simple things," Okera said with a smile.

"That's not much, it's been that hard finding a woman with

Thug Alibi

those few qualities? That's tough. I was sure you were going to add her being a freak to that list, but you've surprised me. You're a good boy, aren't you?" Bria questioned and Okera damn near fell over laughing. The last time he was considered a good boy was when he was a year old.

"What?"

"A good boy? Nah, a freak is definitely a part of my list. My woman has to be able to handle me in bed... I mean, I can be a little much for some. She has to be a beast in the sheets," Okera added with a grin. Bria laughed nervously, she hadn't bedded anyone in a long time. She was no beast, but for as fine as Okera was, she was willing to try. Bria giggled at her thoughts and sipped her wine.

"You good?"

"Yeah, I'm good—oh, here's the main course," Bria said changing the subject quickly. The night seemed to go on forever as the two laughed and talked about life, relationships and their next date.

Once their dinner was done, Okera walked Bria out to the makeshift boardwalk that replaced the sidewalk on the side of the restaurant. The stars glimmered over them, reflecting on the lake as the water lightly crashed against the rocks below them. Okera locked fingers with Bria and spoke in a calm, yet hypnotic tone.

"Xiibria, do you think you could see yourself doing this again?"

"That's very possible. I had a good time, so I don't see why not. Just let me know when you have some free time away from your dating and work."

"I think I can make time for you whenever you're done doing your court thing," Okera said. He knew Bria was lying about being a court officer.

"Good. Well, we're here... thanks again for tonight. I needed this break from work and the craziness in my life," Bria said with an innocent smile as she handed the valet driver her ticket.

"Of course, make sure you call me when you get in so that I can know you made it safely. I know you can handle yourself, but it'll make me feel better," Okera said honestly.

"Sure," she said before she kissed him on the cheek and ducked inside her car the moment the driver got out. She took off into the night leaving Okera there with his feelings. She was nothing like Teva or him. She was classy with a bit of hood sense, it was exactly what he wanted his woman to be like. He turned and made his way to his Bentley, starting towards his house with Bria strutting through his mind. Her fat ass bouncing around underneath her dress while her thick legs teased him.

His phone rung and startled him, he was tripping. *Damn!*

"Wassup Z, what's going on?" Okera said into the phone.

"Nothing, I was just checking up on you. Nigga, you've been off the radar for a few hours now, you good?" Zeke replied.

"Yeah, I had a date."

"A date? Your clown ass still entertaining Teva's lil' thot ass?" Zeke spat.

"Hell nah, I had a date with Bria. Man, shorty is badder than a mufucka! I might have to cuff her on some real shit, I mean for real. She's funny, smart, sexy... damn man, why you ain't tell me she was gon' have a nigga trying to wife her?" Okera exclaimed with a shake of his head.

"Nigga, I didn't know. Until I saw the picture, I thought my girl was trying to hook you up with some ol' mush mouth bitch that works in her salon. You just better be careful with that one, you know what type of background she has. I still can't believe they don't remember you from the club that night."

"We were sitting on the other side of the club. She still doesn't want to tell me what she really does. That's okay though, the truth will come out sooner than later. I can't lie, I'm ready to fuck. This taking my time shit is killing me... I mean she looks like she ain't had no dick in a minute," Okera admitted. Zeke burst into laughter.

"Yo ass crazy. I gotta get back to my girl, I'll holla at you tomorrow."

Okera pulled into the driveway of his house and climbed out of the car. Teva's car was parked in the driveway. The lights in the living room were on, so he knew she was up waiting on him. He had the power on his phone off while he was with Bria to ensure there were no interruptions. The moment he opened the door, Teva stood to her feet and walked over to him with an angry look on her face.

"Where the fuck have you been O?"

"What?" He replied with a disturbed look on his face. It was clear Teva had him fucked up, so he was going to allow her to correct herself.

"Where have you been? I've been waiting on you all night, I thought we were going to have dinner tonight?" Teva asked with sadness.

"I had some business to handle, we'll do that shit another time. Right now, I just want to take a hot shower and get some rest. Goodnight JaTeva," Okera said calmly before brushing her off and going up the stairs.

"Fuck you," Teva said lowly.

"What?" Okera replied.

"Nothing."

~

"Ugh, I can't believe it's already been another murder when we're still backed up on the others. If we don't get one of these solved, Dobbs is going to have our asses," Bria said to Det. Reed, another homicide detective.

"I know, Curt and I have about the same caseload and it's not getting any better. Our informant said that this is a rivalry, but he's been unable to find out the names of the leaders. This is from a different area and he's only been getting bits and pieces from the streets," Reed said as he and Bria walked over to the body.

The man had been strangled to death and pushed between two huge steel dumpsters. This murder was different from any of the other homicides she'd been working. There were no missing limbs and the body wasn't found in a car. This was something else. Bria looked around for any evidence that could give her a lead. She kicked around a few empty potato chip bags and that's when she spotted it. She looked around to make sure no one was looking before she used her pen to pick up the beaded bracelet. Her stomach felt like it had dropped to her asshole. This bracelet was eerily similar to one she'd seen before.

She inspected the bracelet and found a small gold place with "To my baby B," engraved on it. She quickly dropped the bracelet and snapped a picture of it with her phone after she put it exactly where and how it was found. Once that was done, she used her pen again to pick it up and place it in a small evidence bag. She sealed the bag and held it up with terror in her eyes. She was hoping it was just some kind of coincidence or a fluke of some kind.

"Is this our victim?" Bryce said as he walked up behind Bria. She hurried to slip the bag into her pocket and stood to her feet. She had to get her shit together and fast. She didn't want Bryce to become suspicious. She didn't know if he was guilty or not, but she wasn't going to take any chances.

"Yeah, victim looks to be about twenty-five. Our C.O.D (cause of death) looks to be asphyxiation. He was strangled to death with this wife-beater. This is truly sad, he had a baby on the way. The girlfriend already found out and she's over there. We'll have her go down to the morgue for a proper I.D on the victim."

"Alright, seems like you already took care of everything on this one. Dobbs is giving this one to Reed and Curt. So, we can just hand our info over to them," Bryce said anxiously.

"No problem, I need to focus on my own cases anyway. Where the hell have you been?" Bria questioned.

"I was caught up with my young thing. I knew you'd get everything handled," Bryce said coolly.

"Uh huh, you had to drop her off to school? I told you about messing around with those high school girls."

Bria joked with Bryce, but her mind was everywhere. She needed to know if Bryce had anything to do with this murder and if he did, what was the reason behind it. She took her job seriously and this shit was about to put her in a tough spot. Bryce taught her everything she knew about being a great homicide detective.

Damn, do I turn my partner in or am I supposed to cover this shit up?

"Here's everything we have on your case, we have to head back and check on leads for our cases. Good luck," Bryce said cockily.

Bria looked over at him with disgust and before he could question her, her phone chimed with a text.

Okera: *I usually don't act this thirsty, but you've been on my mind all day. How about we hang out tonight, dinner?*

Xiibria: *I have that effect on men. What time?*

Okera: *Ha, 7.*

A huge smile was on Bria's face as she texted back and forth with Okera. She was into him, she was just hoping this was something real. Bryce stared at her before he spoke, jealously forced him to speak without thinking.

"Who the hell got you smiling like that? You must have a date?"

Bria looked at him and turned up her lips before she shook her head.

"It's just Syria, calm down. Let's go."

Bryce turned up his nose at Bria then followed her to the car. He had much more to worry about than who Xiibria was keeping herself busy with. He needed to make sure the case he was building stuck and that no one or nothing got in the way of it.

Chapter Five

Bria sat at her desk contemplating on her next date with Okera. They had been on the phone every night for at least an hour over the past couple weeks. Since he was busy with work, they hadn't seen one another outside of FaceTime, since the double date at Zeke's place. As much as she tried to fight it, Bria was falling for Okera and it made her nervous. Her lil' midday fantasies were cut short when Dobbs stepped out of his office.

"Sams, my office now!"

Her colleagues looked over at her as she stood slowly and made her way into his office, closing the door behind her. She already knew what he wanted, he'd been riding the entire department for the past week. He held out his hand to instruct her to sit in the chair in front of his desk.

"So, how is the investigation going? Have you two got any suspects in mind? I mean, it's been weeks and the community wants some answers. The chief has been on my ass about these murders and I ensured him that my best team was on it."

"Yes sir, I do have a suspect, I just need a name on him. I'm going to meet with my C.I in an hour for more information. Don't worry boss, I should be cracking this case soon enough," Bria said hoping she was right. She had to put her schoolgirl crush aside and get back to work.

"Alright, I'm counting on you. And keep an eye on that partner of yours, he's been a little off lately. I don't know what it is, but with the Feds barging in on these investigations, I can't afford any fuck-ups right now. You're dismissed," Dobbs said as he shifted his attention back to his computer.

"Did you get fired?" Reed said with Curt listening in for an answer as Bria emerged from the office.

"Really you two? No, he just said we all had better start solving these cases. The chief is breathing down his neck and with the Feds trying to make this case a R.I.C.O, we don't have time to waste. Now, stop minding my business and get back to work," Bria commanded before she grabbed her things and headed out, she had a meeting to get to.

She pulled up to an abandoned gas station just outside of the neighborhood where everything had been going down. After putting a rush on her plans, the CI was meeting her there and she was hoping he could give her some valuable information. A tap on the window startled her as she sent kissy face emojis to Okera. She popped the lock and allowed him into the car before she took off with him laying down in the back.

"So, what's up? What do you have for me?" She asked as she glanced at him in the rear-view mirror. Bria analyzed him, using a mental notepad to take notes of the black jeans he wore and the hoodie he had pulled over his head with the strings tightened. Of his face, the only thing she could make out was his nose and his full lips. When her pretty eyes met his, he began to stammer as he spoke.

"Y-you need to talk to this young nigga named Koki. He works in this club over on LaSalle, but, at this time of day it's members only. I suggest you go over there like a civilian... pretend you're some bitch he tried to holla at. Tell him that he told you to come by. That young mufucka is always tipsy and high; he's a playboy. If you go over there like a cop, they're going to shut you down before you even pull up. You don't look like a cop, so you have that working for you," Boo said as he focused his eyes out the window, unlike when he spoke to Bryce. It was something about her eyes that made him nervous.

"Okay, cool. Thanks. Make sure you keep me posted on anything you find out. I need these cases solved sooner than later and I can use all the help I can get. Here," Bria said as she reached back to hand him $300. It was more than she usually gave, but this info was vital to her getting Dobbs off her ass. Boo slipped out the door and was up the street before she could blink her eyes.

Boo was young, about twenty-five to be exact. He had brown skin and dreads that were always neat whenever he wasn't hiding underneath a hoodie. He was very handsome and whenever Bria drove past his block, he would be surrounded by women and young thugs who seemed to look up to him. She shook her head before she took off.

"If only they knew his ass was snitching…"

Bria pulled up a block from the club Boo sent her to and started to remove her holster, gun and badge. She was glad that she decided to dress down that day, it would be more believable. She wore tight blue jeans that hugged her curves and made her already fat ass stand out more. A fitted floral short-sleeved shirt and a pair of pink Huaraches completed her outfit. She pulled the scrunchy from her hair and shook her naturally curly hair loose.

After checking her makeup in the mirror, she climbed out of the car with her phone in her hand. She put on her best ratchet bitch performance and made her way to the front door of the club. She walked up to the man standing outside the club and tried barging her way in.

"Hold up, hold up shorty. The club is open to members only until the club opens at nine," the tall, dark-skinned man said as he held out his buff arm.

"What?! Koki told me to come and see him… I'm just gon' get on the phone and tell him that his people aren't letting me in. I'm sure he won't appreciate y'all standing in the way of him getting some of this good pussy," Bria said with a snap of her neck. She wanted to laugh at how good her acting was, but she had to keep her shit together. The man looked over at his partner that was also guarding the door before he buckled.

"Alright, alright, go in. He's in the back office to the right," the man said as he stepped aside to allow her in. Bria made sure to put a lil' extra stank on her walk as the men watched her go into the club.

"Gaddamn that bitch got a fat ass!"

"Yeah, she's pretty as fuck, she's bad," the other guy said with a shake of his head.

Once she made it past the tables where the members were sitting, drinking and smoking, Bria stank-walked all the way to Koki's office. She eased inside and locked the door behind her then focused her attention on the man in front of her. He was sitting his young, fine ass at the desk smoking a blunt. His sexy brown eyes looked at her, sizing her up from head to toe and back up. His long lashes batted before he bit down on his bottom lip, flexing his dimples; he was impressed. He stood up and Bria thought she would lose it, his body reminded her of Okera's, tall, strong and covered in tattoos.

"Since you locked yourself in here, I'm guessing you want more than to have a conversation with me. My men said that I invited you over, so it had to have been during my drunken state. However, I gotta say you are sexy as hell... I was right to invite you back," Koki said with a sly grin as he walked in front of the desk and leaned back on his hands.

"You know, you should do more business and less talking, you'll get further in life. I came here to ask some questions about these murders that have been plaguing the city," Bria said losing her ratchet tone and becoming more serious.

"Who the fuck are you to be asking me questions?" Koki snapped with anger.

"I'm Detective Sams, Chicago P.D., the homicide division. Now, a little birdie told me that you would have some answers for me. Look, I don't care about what you do here, drugs, women, whatever... all I care about are the bodies that have been turning up all over the city."

"I don't have anything to tell you. I don't know shit about what's been going on. All I know is that I need you to get the fuck out of my spot right now!" Koki shouted. His men unlocked the door with a key and barged inside the office.

"Uh uh, I suggest you two back the fuck up. Koki, we can do this the easy way or the hard way, it's your choice. I just wanna know what's going on?" Bria demanded with a scowl.

"Unless you have a warrant, get the fuck out!"

Bria nodded to let Koki know that she understood him before she backed out of the office and then turned to hurry out. She hadn't gotten anywhere with the information Boo gave her and it was starting to piss her off. The murders were starting to gain more attention from the media and they still didn't have a suspect in custody. Bria made it back to her car then threw her arms over the steering wheel and laid her head down.

"This shit is stressing me the fuck out! I need a drink," she said aloud as she turned the key. After finding some music to help tune out her reality, Bria took off towards the nearest store to purchase an expensive bottle of wine. That cheap shit wouldn't suffice.

Bria changed into her jogging attire and started along her trail. She didn't know why her run helped to ease her mind of the stress her job encompassed, but she was glad it helped. Her phone chimed the second she stepped foot on her porch. It was Syria asking how her day was and if she was still into Okera.

Bria: *Work has been a pain in my ass today, I'm so glad to be off for the next couple of days. And... yes, I am talking to Okera. I want to see him again, but it's like he's always inviting me out and trying to help me feel better. I feel like such a burden.*

Syria: *Girl please! Let that nigga wine and dine you, you deserve it. If you want to stop feeling like a "burden," I suggest inviting him over for dinner tomorrow. That'll give you time to plan out a sexy dinner and get you some lingerie for dessert.*

Bria: *Yeah, that sounds like a good idea. Wait, lingerie?!*

Syria: *Bitch, as fine as that nigga is... you need to be fucking to make sure he's worth your time. Stop being so damn stuck-up. Now, if you need any tips let me know, I got you.*

Bria shook her head and laughed at her friend. She had a point, but thinking about Okera in that way made her nervous. She tossed her phone aside then headed to the bathroom to shower. Bria synced her phone to the Sony Speaker in her bathroom and allowed Pandora to set the tone. She pulled off her clothes and stepped in under the hot water, closing the door behind her. The bathroom began to steam up and so did the playlist.

"Damn, okay Pandora!" Bria shouted as Jeremih's "Forever, I'm Ready" made images of Okera pop into her mind. She could only imagine how sexy he was with his clothes off. That was one man she wouldn't mind dominating her.

Her hands wandered over her body as the suds slid down her smooth caramel skin. Before she knew what was happening she had rubbed herself into an orgasm. Her phone rung over the speaker and made her head snap forward with embarrassment. *Shit!*

Bria quickly washed her body and her hair before she stepped out and wrapped herself up in a towel. She didn't know who was calling her, but she was glad they didn't interrupt her nut, she needed that. The phone went off again and her face began to glow once she realized who was calling; it was Okera.

"Hey!" Bria panted in an exasperated tone.

"Hey beautiful. You're breathing kinda heavy… you must've been thinking about me?" Okera joked causing Bria to chuckle nervously. If only he knew.

"You wish; how was your day?" She replied, jumping the subject.

"It was good, the builders have already started remodeling the hotel in L.A. and I couldn't be more excited. How was your day?" He replied.

"Honestly, it was horrible. I'm just hoping I can unwind this weekend and forget about work… I had an idea; how about you come over tomorrow evening and I'll cook dinner for us. You're always going all out for me and I think you deserve a nice night of being catered to," Bria said with a sly grin. She was hornier than she was in the shower.

"Hmm, I like being catered to. Should I bring anything?"

"Just yourself and that handsome smile. Oh, it's casual so, a nice pair of jeans and a shirt will do. I want to see what you look like when you're not making money."

"I can do that and maybe bring a little something extra for the night," Okera crooned and suddenly Bria could feel her essence began to seep. He had to laugh a bit at the dress code for dinner; he made money in his sleep so there was nothing he could wear that he didn't make money in.

"That's what's up, so I'll see you tomorrow at 7 sharp. Don't be late," Bria said before ending the call.

She laid back on the bed like a teenage girl in love. The big smile on her face turned into a frown when the doorbell chimed. Bria looked over at the clock.

"8:15, I don't care; it's still too late for uninvited guest."

She tied the belt on her robe and allowed her damp hair to swing freely over her shoulders. She crept down the stairs with her mace in her pocket and eased up to the door. A quick glance through the window beside the door and an eyeroll later, she quickly figured out who was bothering her. Bria snatched open the door and leaned on one leg as she sized Bryce up.

"Hey Bria, what's up?"

"Hey? How can I help you?" Bria asked suspiciously.

"I need to talk to you about these cases we have and fill you in on some new information. Can I come in?" Bryce asked as he held up a file folder.

"Sure, come in," Bria replied curiously. If he had something that could help them get their cases solved and get Dobbs off their ass, she was all for it.

Bryce walked in and glanced around Bria's living room that was decorated with white leather furniture, royal-blue accents and gold trims. It was different from the last time he'd been there. In the past, he would come over to hang with Moses until he and Bria ended it. He looked over at Bria with thirsty eyes as her robe opened a bit, exposing cleavage. Her long hair was flipped over to one side as she looked through the folder. Bryce bit down on his bottom lip before he redirected his attention to her face.

"So, Koki's gang is behind the murders? Is he our suspect?" Bria asked anxiously.

"Yes, we need to get more evidence on him in order for us to get a warrant."

"But, he doesn't match the description of our suspect…"

"I believe Koki has been having someone else to handle the dirty work. Anyway, he's not even the real culprit, he's mid-level. It's his boss that we want. But, I'll be working hard on this while you enjoy your weekend," Bryce said with a grin.

"Uh huh, I can't believe you have time for work with all the lil' girl chasing you've been doing," Bria replied slyly. Bryce shot daggers at her before he came back with a smart remark.

"Nah, but if you keep looking like this, I'll be chasing after you… Well, I gotta get to work, I'll keep you updated on everything," Bryce said as he stood up from the couch and grabbed the folder. Bria kept her face normal, but in her head, she was trying to figure out when in fact did Bryce start crushing on her. She tried to pretend like she didn't notice, but his eyes had been wandering lately.

"Bye," Bria said before closing the door. She turned around and leaned up against it with a confused look on her face before shaking her head and retreating to her bedroom. She had better things to worry about, like what she was making Okera for dinner the next day.

The next day, Bria headed to the store to pick up the ingredients for dinner. She was making red wine spaghetti with crumbled spicy meatballs; it was one of her new favorite dishes to make. She found the recipe online one day and fell in love with the flavors. There was no doubt in Bria's mind that Okera would love it. Italian food was his favorite. She was pairing it with a fresh baked Italian loaf coated with garlic butter and three cheeses. Bria's phone chimed as she walked through the aisles picking up the things she would need.

"Hello?"

"Hey boo! Are you ready for tonight?" Syria asked, clearly wearing a grin.

"Yes, I can't wait until he tastes this pasta and…"

"And that pussy. Ooh, I can't wait until you get you some dick, friend. You've been acting like a straight lame lately, Okera needs to loosen you up," Syria said honestly.

Bria had to laugh at how crazy her friend was, but she couldn't lie and say that she wasn't curious. She had the house spotless and smelling good. The day seemed to have flown by; it was already four in the afternoon and Bria was whipping in the kitchen with a mission.

∼

"Yeah, make sure y'all get the blocks hemmed up, but don't play that shit too close. You know those puss ass detectives have been snooping around my spot. Keep this shit clean," Gahd said as he shouted out commands for his crew.

"We got it," the crew said before they exited the room. Zeke stayed behind to talk with his friend. It had been a couple days since they'd spoken about anything outside of work and their new business ventures. Gahd looked different... happier.

"So... what's been up with you these past few days; you've been kind of short with me? We're still boys outside of this work shit, right?" Zeke asked with a lifted brow.

"Hell yeah, you're my brother. What are you talking about?"

"Don't tell me Teva got your ass on a short leash now. You've been dipping out fast as hell lately."

"Nah bruh, I've been giving Bria all of my free time lately. It's hard having a girl at home and a potential main bitch on the side. Shorty is like none of the bitches and hoes I've fucked with in the past. She's cooking dinner for me tonight at her place… It's crazy; you already know the type of nigga I am, but shorty makes me nervous. I feel like everything has to be perfect for her, for real," Gahd admitted with a bit of puppy love dripping from his words.

"Damn G, shorty done got in your head like that? You in love, bruh?" Zeke asked with a chuckle.

"Nah, not yet, but shit, if the pussy is as good as her conversation and her look then I might be," Gahd admitted before the pair

Thug Alibi

erupted with laughter. Zeke shook his head at the mere thought of his boy being in love. He'd never seen Gahd in love; he would always say that he cared for some women or even had love for them, but in love? Never.

"So, what about Teva? Does she know anything about this "dinner?"

"Hell no. You already know shorty would blow a fuse if she found out I was spending time with another female. She's been a little preoccupied with this school shit, thank God. Otherwise, she'd be all in my face trying to figure out who I'm texting," Gahd admitted in a huff.

"You texting? Teva must've stopped going through your phone?"

"Of course not, I got an identical phone for Bria. I put a lil' dot on it to make sure I know which one is which. I gotta go over here right now to feed her some bullshit about why I can't spend our date night with her. I gotta make her ass study or some shit, but I'll holla at you," Gahd said before shaking Zeke's hand and dismissing himself. He smiled and shook his head again. Zeke had a feeling that Bria was the one. However, he didn't have time to entertain this newfound love story of his friend's, he had his own lover to tend to.

~

Gahd pushed his Bentley coupe at maximum speeds to make it home. He needed to change clothes, lie to Teva and stop to bring a dinner gift for Bria. As he opened the front door, the smell of the Dolce & Gabbana Light Blue perfume Teva wore permeated the air and made him grin. It was the same perfume she wore the first day they met. He fell in love with it until he got a whiff of the Chanel perfume Bria wore. That shit made his dick hard.

"Hey babe, how was work?" Teva asked as if Gahd worked a normal nine to five.

"Work was good, everything has been quiet, and money is still pouring in, so I'm happy. How was school yesterday?" He replied honestly interested. By the time he made it home the night before, Teva was asleep.

"It was cool, I thought that I would feel out of place and that the work would be too hard, but I made it through. So, what do you have planned for our date tonight?" Teva asked with a grin. As much as Gahd was going to hate to let her down, thinking about Bria made it easy.

"Babe, I'm sorry, I gotta handle some business and I won't be back until tomorrow. I tried to get Z to do it for me, but that nigga's all boo'd up," Gahd lied without batting an eye.

"Damn, I was really looking forward to spending some time with you. We've both been so busy… I feel like we never see each other anymore," Teva whined with a pout.

"Tomorrow night, it's going to be me and you, whatever you want, okay?"

Teva smiled and nodded in agreement before she fixed her mouth to ask for money.

"Baby, can I have some money to get something to eat, maybe catch a movie or something, since I have to take myself on a date?"

He already knew what she was trying to do; hang out with her messy ass friends to get drunk and high. He tossed her $500 and headed to the bathroom to shower. Gahd wanted to keep his conversation with Teva short to avoid her trying to get some dick. She had a habit of trying him before he went out. He looked at it as her way of trying to "drain him" so no other bitch could fuck him, but she of all people should've known better than that. He was proud of what he had, his stamina couldn't be tamed, and one nut didn't stop no show with Gahd.

Once he stepped out of the shower, he tied a towel around his waist and wiped the steam from the mirror. A sly smile revealed that gorgeous white grill that Bria loved and the dimples that complemented it. He brushed his teeth and then his waves before spraying on his Tom Ford cologne and applying the matching body lotion. Through the bedroom and straight to the closet, Gahd traveled as Teva looked on to scope him out. He was glad the dress code for today was relaxed; she'd be all in his shit if he pulled out a suit and tie. Gahd grabbed a pair of blue jeans and a white and blue slim-fitting tee and matched it up with a pair of wheat Tims.

Teva's eyes were trained on him like a watch dog until her phone went off. He quickly slid on his diamond chain and tucked it in before he put on a simple Audemars watch. She knew he didn't like wearing jewelry unless he was going somewhere special. He was dressed down and he couldn't wait to see what Bria was wearing. He slid his wallet in his back pocket along with his phone before tucking his pistol in his back.

"Alright babe, I'm out of here. Wish me luck," Gahd said with a sly grin.

"Luck? What kind of business deal are you going to dressed like that?" Teva questioned with attitude.

"You already know, so why the fuck would you ask that dumb ass question. See you tomorrow," Gahd said with a snarl before he hurried out of the house. He hopped in his Bentley and pulled out his "Bria" phone and read the message she sent.

Bria: *Dinner's almost ready, I'll see you in an hour.*

Okera: *I can't wait to taste you… it. Sorry.*

Bria sent a splash emoji and then the smiley face with heart eyes. That slip-up was unintentional, but if she was on the menu, he was more than willing to try it. He took off towards the wine store he frequented to grab a bottle of his favorite red wine. It was expensive, delicious and could get you in the right mood. Okera always said that it was a reminiscent of himself.

Once the wine was purchased, he was on his way to Bria. As soon as he pulled into her driveway, his phone went off. It was Teva texting him on his other phone. He closed his eyes and shook his head before he read the message.

Teva: *Babe, is it okay if I invite a few of the girls over. I promise to make them smoke outside.*

Gahd: *Yeah, that's cool. Just make sure those lil' nasty bitches don't fuck up my house and it better be spotless when I get back.*

Teva: *Thank you, baby. And why you gotta talk about my friends like that?*

Gahd: *BYE!*

He tossed the phone inside his glove box then took a deep

breath to get his head right before he approached Bria. *That damn girl.*

Okera grabbed the bottle of wine and then made his way up the stairs. He checked out his reflection in the window to make sure he was on point before he pressed the doorbell a few times to let her know her savior had arrived.

Inside, Bria was scrambling to straighten everything in her path as she hurried to the front of the house. She stopped to assess herself in the mirror that hung on the wall next to her.

"Damn, I'm fine," she said aloud before she adjusted her dress and then pulled open the door.

She couldn't hide how big her eyes got as she looked at Okera with lustful eyes. The t-shirt he wore was loose in the waist and slightly fitted in the chest, but his muscular arms gave the sleeves a stretch. It was something about a sexy nigga in Timberland boots that drove her crazy. She blamed it on her New York rapper crushes she had as a teenage girl. His handsome face and those bedroom eyes had her stumbling to get her words out.

"C-come in, I'm glad you could make it," Bria stammered before she licked her lips. She always struggled to hide her thoughts.

"Thank you. Damn, you look amazing," Okera crooned as he eyed Bria. She sported a royal-blue bodycon dress that stopped mid-thigh. It hugged her curves like a spoiled kid on his mom's leg and the shit wouldn't quit. Her toned legs were oiled to perfection, while her pretty toes, peeked through the heels she wore.

"Thank you," Bria said shyly as she tossed her long hair back out of her face.

"I thought we were dressing down?" Okera questioned curiously.

"I am dressed down, this is a t-shirt dressed. I'm not wearing any fancy jewelry… it's the shoes, right? I'm sorry, I'll take them off—"

"Nah, leave 'em on," Okera said slyly. His eyes screamed I wanna fuck you in those heels and Bria's pussy was ready to oblige.

"Okay… well, follow me. The dining room is this way, and everything is all ready for you."

Thug Alibi

"Before I forget, here you go. It's already chilled, we can drink it now or later."

"Ooh, this is that expensive shit. Damn, we went all out huh?" Bria teased as she eyeballed the bottle.

"$250 for a bottle of wine? That's chump change, I spend that on a couple pairs of underwear. Money is not an issue with me love, but you'll find that all out in due time. And I'm a gentleman; the woman should always be seated first," Okera said sternly. He wasn't just putting on for Bria; he treated Teva the same way. He was raised to treat his woman like a queen; spoil her, pull out her chair, open doors for her. His father didn't play when it came to schooling his sons on how to be a true ladies' man.

Bria smiled as she sat down in the chair across from Okera. She had already plated the salad when she heard him pull up in the driveway, so they were good to go. An ice-cold glass of wine and another of water sat in front of them, with fine china sporting the beautiful salad she'd taken her time to prepare.

Okera stuck a forkful of the salad in his mouth and his eyes lit up. He followed that one with another before Bria felt the need to question the look on his face.

"How is it?"

"This is delicious; what kind of dressing is this?" Okera asked anxiously. His love for food was the reason he ran two successful restaurants.

"It's homemade; I used a red wine vinegar, oil and added my own special seasonings. Do you really like it? It's been a minute since I've cooked for anyone other than myself or Syria," Bria asked nervously.

"Yes, I love this. If this is your own recipe, you should think about bottling this shit and selling it. You'd make a killing," Okera said honestly.

"Thank you," Bria said with a smile.

Okera nodded his head as he continued to enjoy his salad, making sure to save some room for the main dish and afterwards, dessert. Once they were done Bria took up the plates and then came back with the pasta dish she'd worked so hard on. It looked like something out of a cookbook, delicious and beautifully plated.

"Damn, you sure you made this? I'm not going to go in the kitchen and find some boxes or no shit like that, am I?" Okera joked making Bria laugh.

"Of course not, I made all of this. Now, enjoy," Bria said as she sat the food down in front of him and hurried to join. She watched his face as he stuck the pasta into his mouth and savored it. He took a bite of the bread next and his eyes began to glaze over.

"You okay?" Bria asked hoping he wasn't disappointed.

"Oh my God, it's official... I'm claiming you, so you gotta cut all of your other niggas off," Okera joked as he licked his lips. Bria erupted with laughter before she shook her head, his response was enough for her.

"I'm glad I could snatch you up with just one meal. So Okera, tell me how your dating has been going... or are you still dating?"

"I gotta be honest, I haven't been dating anyone outside of you and one other person. The other woman, she and I have been dating for some months."

"So, she's your girlfriend?" Bria asked with a bit of hostility.

"No, I thought she could be, but as of late, she's been proving otherwise. She's very immature and she lacks goals...ambition. I need a woman who's on the same level as I am mentally," Gahd admitted. He had to omit the part about he and Teva staying together or them being in a relationship for a year. He was about to end it anyway, so he didn't feel the need to reveal all of that.

"I see. Well, you have to do what you have to do. If you both are on the same page when it comes to exclusivity, then you should be good." Bria was hoping that shit was a wrap. Okera had to be hers and hers alone.

"Thanks. I know you had a bad break a year ago, but what's been holding you back from dating?"

"Work and fear. I'm afraid of being hurt again. There's something about you that makes me want to take a chance and I'm hoping it was a good choice," Bria revealed enjoying their conversation. It was the first time that the two had let all of their truths out... so she thought.

A short time later, dinner was over and now it was time for dessert. Bria invited Okera into the living room where she had the central air blasting to combat the early summer heat and the fireplace burning to set the mood. She knew exactly what she was doing. She grabbed the expensive bottle of wine and two glasses, along with a bowl of sweet, sliced strawberries. Bria bought a few tubs of Hennessy infused whipped cream for the night and she was hoping they'd be drunk in love by the end of the night.

Her nerves were all over the place as she walked into the living room where Okera waited. He sat on the plush rug in front of the fireplace while his eyes followed Bria into the room. He hopped to his feet to grab the items from her and sat them on the table behind him as he helped her down to the floor. She picked up her iPod from the table and turned on her playlist of slow songs.

"This is nice, I haven't had a romantic night like this in a long time or a woman as beautiful as you to spend it with. Let me," Okera said as he reached for the bottle and popped the cork. He poured each of them a hefty glass of the wine before he grabbed the bowl of strawberries. He watched as Bria took a sip of the wine then nodded her head with approval.

"I'm glad I decided to do this... this is fun," Bria said with a grin. The wine from dinner paired with the gulps of the expensive wine she was drinking had her tipsy.

"Me too. I'm really feeling you B and I'm hoping this can go much further. I don't just wanna date you, I want you to be my woman... all mine," Okera admitted. She had him open and he was beginning to show his true colors. He had to reel it in a bit to prevent himself from revealing too much. He was a thug ass nigga that knew how to class it up like the perfect gentleman.

"Damn..." Bria replied with shock.

"That's not what you're looking for, huh?" Okera replied in a defeated tone.

"Nah, it's exactly what I'm looking for. It's just... I feel like you're too good to be true. I've always settled when I got into my past relationships. He wouldn't have a job, he'd have baby mama drama, or he was a hoe... you know, shit like that. But with you, I haven't seen any of those things. O, I'm scared," Bria admitted.

Okera leaned over and kissed Bria gently on the lips, sucking the wine off. He grabbed a strawberry then rubbed the juice on her lips before he allowed her to eat. He licked her lips before he began to suck on them, using his tongue to make love to her mouth.

Damn, this nigga can kiss the draws off a bitch, Bria thought to herself. She could feel her juices leaking between her thick thighs and suddenly she remembered she wasn't wearing underwear. Okera pulled back to observe her reaction; she was squirming in the tiny dress and he was ready to take it off. However, he was going to play his position, so he sat back and allowed her to take control.

"Don't worry B, I'm going to take care of you in every way possible; mentally, physically, emotionally, and financially. I got you, shorty, and I'm not playing," Okera admitted allowing a bit of Gahd to slip out.

"I like that..." Bria said with a bite of her bottom lip.

"What?" Okera said with a look of confusion.

"I like when you talk like that; that thug shit turns me on. I guess you can blame it on me hanging in the hood when I was younger and all the trap music I listen to now," Bria said shyly.

"Come here," Okera said as he eyed Bria seductively. She crawled over to him trying to be as sexy as possible. The deep plunging neckline allowed Okera to view her breasts with no problem. She wasn't wearing a bra.

He pulled her chin up to him and kissed her lips passionately. Bria thirstily reached over and grabbed his shirt, pulling it over his head to expose his chest. It was just as she imagined, covered in tattoos and rippled with muscles. Just the look of him had her wet.

"Damn, you got a body fit for a God," Bria said softly causing Okera to chuckle at the reference. If she only knew that she was about to feel exactly what the body of Gahd could do. Bria rubbed her hands down his chest and admired the tattoos on his skin.

"You like that?" Okera asked as he looked down at Bria admiring his art.

"Yeah, I love it," Bria said before she tugged at Okera's jeans, undoing the top button. She was thirsty, and he could tell. It had been over a year since she'd had any penetration and her pussy was purring.

He gently pushed her back then grabbed the bottom of her dress before hesitating a bit. He was sure that she wanted to go further, but he was afraid to push. *Fuck it!* He began to lift her dress over her head and was shocked at the sight before him. Bria sat buck bald naked with only her heels on. He stood to his feet and stepped back a bit, stepping out of his shoes and admired Bria. He lifted the chains from his neck and removed his watch, setting them down on the table with his eyes still focused on the task at hand, Bria. She stood up and allowed Okera to view her freshly waxed pussy and her supple breasts that sat up perfectly.

"Damn, shorty... you're bad!" Okera admitted as he stood at attention in more ways than one. Bria strutted over in her heels with her hips swaying to the sounds of Tank crooning "Sexy."

I've been thinkin' bout you all day
Thinkin' bout you feel like foreplay, Sexy
Don't know how much that I'm gon' take
If it's mine, then baby, don't play, Sexy

She bit down on her bottom lip seductively as she continued over to him. Roughly, she grabbed his jeans and unzipped them before pulling them and his boxers down. Her eyes grew as she eyed his thick, long dick that pointed at her; she was chosen.

Okera picked her up then laid her on the rug in front of the fireplace. The flicker of the flames reflected on her oiled skin. She was beautiful, and the innocent look on her face made her look sexier. He started from her lips, kissing his way down to her neck and then between her breasts. He gripped them both, rubbing the nipples before he sucked on each one gently with soft tongue swirls.

"Ooh O, that shit feels so good," Bria moaned softly. The music provided the perfect backdrop for the visual in the room. Her heart raced as Okera moved on, continuing to kiss down to her navel and then her swollen mound of caramel skin.

"Damn, you smell so good, I bet you taste even better," Okera crooned then licked his lips. Using his tongue, he parted her lips going straight for her clit. His tongue flickered to the rhythm of the music before he began to suck on it. He slipped the middle and ring fingers of his right hand into her mouth, signaling for her to suck on them. Bria did just that in between soft moans.

He pulled his fingers from her mouth and used them to loosen up her tightness as he pushed inside her. He could feel exactly how long it had been since she'd made love and it caused his dick to get a little harder at the thought of her not being able to handle him.

"Shit... mm!" Bria moaned.

"That pretty pussy is so tight," Okera whispered then continued to drive Bria wild with the bomb head he was giving her. Her nails scratched his scalp when his fingers reached her g-spot and began to strum her like a tune on a guitar. Bria fought to hold onto the nut that had been bottled up all night, but she couldn't control herself.

"GOD!" Bria shouted as she shook on his fingers and came in his mouth, feeding his hunger. A smile crept on his face at the sound of her unknowingly screaming his street name aloud. After about a minute, Bria popped up and went for what she wanted as Okera sat back on his knees in front of her. She took his thick dick into her hands then kissed the head before engulfing him with her mouth. It had been so long since she'd given head, so she coached herself through the act, not forgetting to flex the skills she'd once perfected.

"Fuuck!" Okera shouted as he looked down at Bria sucking his dick better than the bitch he had waiting at home. He was turned on by how good she was and how sexy she looked but disgusted at how terrible Teva's head was compared to Bria. He had found his wifey and he was hoping that by the morning she would be allowing him to lay claim to her.

Before he could climax, Okera stopped Bria and pushed her back on the floor. He grabbed a Magnum from the pocket of his jeans, easing it on his dick as he sucked on her pussy once more to get it wetter. With those sexy bedroom eyes, he looked up at Bria and then kissed her. She was already falling; the way he handled her was different from Moses.

He slid into her and her eyes began to roll around in her head.

Okera's dick stretched her out, giving her both pleasure and pain. Once she adjusted to his size, Okera sat back on his knees pushing her legs out into a split while he fucked her into back to back orgasms.

"O, O, oh my God!" Bria cried out with another climax. Okera was tired of being gentle; he was ready to show her why women loved to call him Gahd. He flipped her onto her stomach and kissed down her back gently before he slid into her.

"Shit, it's so big!" Bria grunted as she forced herself to handle Okera. She tried to keep him at bay, but the powerful orgasms he caused made her arms weak. He lifted her on all fours then pushed her shoulders down to the floor.

"Face down, ass up!" Okera commanded while slapping her ass. He was becoming rough and it turned her on more. He dug deeply into her and he couldn't hold out any longer.

"God, Oh God," was all Bria could muster.

"Shit, I'm bout to cum!" He shouted before he exploded then laid on top of her before rolling over. His eyes were fixed on the ceiling while wearing a smile on his face.

"Damn, you gon' have a nigga wifin' you up," he said, still smiling. Bria didn't say a word. Okera started to regret what he said, maybe he had gotten a little too comfortable around Bria. He took her silence as her way of disagreeing until he looked over and realized she had fallen fast asleep. He chuckled a bit before he reached over and pulled the throw blanket from the couch and snuggled underneath it with Bria. She turned over and laid on his chest with a smile on her face; he had done his job.

Chapter Six

"Wassup Jo!" A young guy said as he walked up to shake Carti's hand.

"Sup fam, it's been a minute since I've seen you out here. What's been up with you?" He replied with sincerity while gazing down the block.

"Shit man, I just came home a few days ago. I'm trying to get my hustle up, so I can be riding around in some shit like this one day," the man said as he eyed the red Wraith Carti was leaning on.

"I told you to get up with me and I'll put you on. You know it ain't shit to look out for my lil' niggas out here. You gotta stop fuckin' with those niggas that mean you no good and link up with some paper chasers. Here, hit me up when you're ready to win," Carti said as he handed the young man a business card. He took the card and nodded his head before walking up the street. He and his right-hand Zero continued to talk with one of the block boys about their moves for the rest of the night.

"Nigga, I'm trying to get up in something wet tonight," Lil' Corey, one of the block boys, said as he puffed on the blunt of kush. He handed Carti the blunt and watched the girls walking up the block.

"I feel you on that and these hoes are trying to be chosen," Zero said before they started to laugh.

Carti quietly leaned against the car with his eyes strolling up and down the block, keeping watch for twelve (police) and his enemies. It was damn near midnight and the young thots were still patrolling. They spoke and switched their asses in front of Carti as they watched him with dollar signs in their eyes. He wore a fitted white tee with two diamond necklaces dangling from his neck. His dreads were neatly braided to the back, allowing his handsome freckled face to be admired by the thirsty block bitches.

His brown eyes looked right over the girls that stood before him and focused on two women that emerged from a BMW coupe. He recognized the walk from anywhere and as they got closer a smirk formed on his face. It was the love of his life and he didn't care what it took, he was going to get her back.

"Hey Carti," Teva said with a smile as her eyes sparkled under the streetlights. They were red and glazed over from the weed she smoked before she hit the block.

"Wassup shorty," Carti replied.

"Nothing much, just hanging out with my girl," she replied, not taking her eyes off Carti.

"Where are you from lil' mama? I've never seen you over here before," Lil' Corey asked thirstily.

"I'm from out south and my name is Lea, not lil' mama," she wasn't paying the guy any attention; she was more interested in Zero. He was dark-skinned and sexy with a low-cut that was drenched in waves. His clothing was similar to Carti's; however, he was taller with muscles for days. His chest flexed as he grabbed the blunt from Carti and watched the girl admire him. He was a bit interested.

"I'm surprised that clown ass nigga of yours doesn't have you somewhere locked down," Carti said as he walked up on Teva. Her eyes roamed his body as memories of her making love to him flashed in her mind. The tattoo of her name on the front of his neck caused butterflies to flicker in her stomach. It had been well over a year and he was still sporting her name as if it was a branding.

"Nah, he had to handle some business tonight, so he won't be back until tomorrow," Teva said vindictively, thinking about how Gahd flaked on what was supposed to be their date night. She made sure to get as high as possible. She was going to enjoy her night one way or another.

"So, what you trying to be on?" Carti asked. He was going to take advantage of the time Teva had. His feelings for her never changed, despite her leaving him for Gahd. Carti couldn't blame her for leaving him after he fucked around on her with two of her friends. The power he had in his hood had him in the streets wildin' and he didn't give a fuck. Teva's eyes shifted from Carti to the nigga standing behind him and suddenly, her mood changed.

"I can't. I gotta go handle something right quick. I'll get up with you another time," Teva said as her eyes shot daggers at Zero. She looked back over at Carti and shot a quick smile before she grabbed her girl and hurried back over to her car.

"Damn, she got out here fast when she spotted you. You fucked before?" Lil' Corey said as he puffed on the blunt and laughed.

"Nigga, hell nah! That's Carti's old bitch... I don't know why he start acting like a lame when that hoe comes around. That hoe left you for your enemy and you're still entertaining thoughts of fucking with her?" Zero gritted with a shake of his head before he grabbed the blunt from Corey.

"Shorty was a real one... I just fucked it all up on some dumb shit. That's my fault. I can't blame her for that," Carti admitted.

"Whatever. Say what you want, but you can't trust a bitch like her," Zero said with a snarl.

"Nigga, you've been knowing me since we were kids. I don't trust these hoes... especially not that one."

"Yeah, alright," Zero said not believing the bullshit his friend was feeding him. His phone rung before he could talk anymore shit to Carti. He answered and said a few words before ending the call and dismissing Lil' Corey.

"Aye, we need to talk business right quick. We'll get up with you in a minute," Zero said before he and Carti shook Corey's hand and watched him disappear into the night.

"Wassup fam?" Carti asked seriously.

"You know that lil' nigga Boo from up the block?" Zero asked with a murderous look in his eyes.

"Yeah, that's my guy... what about him?" Carti replied with confusion.

"Well, 'your guy' has been running his mouth to the police. He's been telling them our moves and he's basically exposed all of our spots out here in these streets. Now, I gotta have all my niggas move around to shake the trail."

"What? That can't be right; my nigga has never been anything other than loyal to me. This has got to be a mistake," Carti replied with a bit of hurt in his voice. He had known Boo since he was a lil' nigga, running around the hood messing with all the girls. Carti had been looking out for him since his brother got killed eight years prior.

"Look at this," Zero said as he showed Boo getting out of an unmarked police car. The face of the officer couldn't be seen, but the moment Boo made it up the block and under the streetlights, he removed his hood, his face could be seen as clear as day.

"Damn," Carti said with a shake of his head.

"Don't worry, bruh, I'm going to handle this lil' nigga," Zero said in a matter of fact tone.

"Nah, I gotta be the one to do this. I can't believe this nigga crossed me. I gotta get out of here," Carti said before he hopped in the coupe and sped off. The murderous look on Zero's face melted into a blank stare as he watched the red car disappear down the street.

∼

"Shit, B, you've been smiling all morning. I take it you had a good weekend?" Bryce asked attempting to pry into Bria's business.

"Don't worry about all of that. Have you gotten anywhere with our suspect?" Bria asked switching subjects.

"I—" Bryce started before a call came in.

"That's us," Bria said as the pair grabbed their things and made their way out of the precinct. They hopped into their car and hurried over to the crime scene, hoping to finally get evidence they can use. Once they arrived on the scene, the patrol officers gave them a briefing on the incident.

"The victim is twenty-five-year-old Tevin "Boo" Lewis. He was shot once in the back of the head and left here on this bench. He was found about thirty minutes ago by that older woman over there; she was walking her dog here in the park."

Both Bria and Bryce had a look of shock covering their faces. It was their C.I. Boo who was murdered and for the first time in a long time, the pair felt the same way. Boo was young, and they felt like he had so much potential. Unlike many of the other thugs in the hood, he had gone to college and graduated with a Bachelor's in Finance. No matter how many times Bria told him that he should leave the street life alone, Boo would only fan her off and tell her that he was good.

"Damn, he was so damn young," Bryce said showing more emotion than Bria had seen from him in a long time.

"Yeah, he was... we gotta solve this. He's always gone out of his way to help us with our cases. That's the least we can do since it's probably our fault that he's dead," Bria admitted.

Bryce quietly nodded his head before they broke to canvas the neighborhood. They had to go all in for Boo. His death, not only hurt both of their feelings, but it was also going to hurt the investigations they were working on. Boo was the one who gave them the suspect information and they needed him to solidify their moves.

Later, the partners were back at the precinct going over witness statements and working hard to get any evidence found on the scene processed. A look of defeat covered their faces while their colleagues joked and laughed behind them. They didn't have time to play; they asses were about to be on the hook for the "Limb Murders."

"Are y'all going to work all night? It's time to go," Det. Reed asked as he and Curt walked out of the office. Their shifts were over.

"Nah, I'm leaving. There's nothing else we can do tonight,

Bryce, are you coming?" Bria asked as she grabbed her things to leave out with the other detectives.

"Yeah, I need to go get some fresh air," Bryce replied as he hurried out behind them brushing past the federal officers and the detectives walking in to start their shifts.

"B, go home and get some rest. Tomorrow, we'll tackle this head-on," Bria said with a smile as she patted her partner on the shoulder. Bryce watched as she switched off to her car and took off. He was going to worry about crushing on her later. In the meantime, he needed to make a run.

A short time later, Bryce was pulling up to Carti's house. He blew out in a huff before he exited the car and made his way over to the door. One of Carti's goons pulled the door open for him and allowed him into the house. As usual, Bryce walked through the house, finding Carti sitting in the entertainment room. The room was lit by red lights and was filled with weed smoke. He and a few of his niggas puffed on blunts as they looked on at two naked bitches dancing to Jacquees' songs.

"Ah shit, my nigga is here!" Carti shouted as he leaned up to shake Bryce's hand.

"Wassup. Aye, I need to holla at you about something really quick," Bryce said with a serious face. Carti finally took his eyes off the hoes in front of him and caught a glimpse of the look on Bryce's face. He stood up and led Bryce out to his office, closing the door behind them.

"Damn nigga, what's wrong?" Carti asked still puffing on his blunt.

"Look, the lil' nigga that was keeping his eye to the streets for me has been killed. All of the intel we have on Gahd thus far came from him. Shit, what are we supposed to do now?" Bryce questioned nervously.

"We'll figure that shit out. Right now, I'm about to get back out here to these bitches. I'm trying to get some pussy," Carti said nonchalantly.

"Damn, you don't give a fuck that we have another hurdle blocking us from taking that nigga out?" Bryce spat with anger.

"Snitches come and go, that lil' nigga just had to meet his maker a lil' sooner than later," Carti said with a laugh. The smug look on his face had only enraged Bryce more. He realized that his search for Boo's killer had come to an end; it was Carti.

"How the fuck can you risk everything we're doing right now by killing Boo? And for what?!" Bryce shouted.

"Nigga, I do what the fuck I want. This is my shit!" Carti barked with rage.

"You need to be more careful out here. Stop running around like a reckless fucking thug, keep this shit clean until we get those cases closed. I'd hate to have to bring your ass in for being a dumb ass nigga," Bryce argued.

"Who do you think you are? Nigga, I'm the one that brought you on… I'm the reason that your pig ass is living the good life. That pussy ass police money ain't doing shit for you, I am! Don't ever in your life try to check me on what the fuck I'm doing. I'm the king of this shit out here!" Carti roared with his chest puffed out. Bryce had struck a nerve and caused Carti to speak to him like he did his low-level block boys.

"Yeah, alright. Just remember the Feds are all over these cases and the last thing you need right now is a federal charge. I'll holla at you later," Bryce said before he exited the office and then Carti's house. Carti leaned back in his chair still puffing his blunt with a scowl. He knew that killing Boo would cause a rift in his plans, but he couldn't allow a muthafucka to think that crossing him came without consequences.

"Daddy, are you going to come back to play with us?" The naked woman said as she walked into the office and dropped to her knees in front of Carti. She freed his dick from his pants and began to suck him like her life depended on it. The look on his face softened a bit, but the conversation he'd just had and the night he murdered Boo were still plaguing his mind.

You're a boss I wanna treat you
I know you tired of all the leeches

∽

Gahd sat in his office going over the final arrangements for the grand opening of his hotel in L.A. He was opening that weekend and had already booked up the hotel for the week. He was now a different type of boss. He was well on his way with his mogul shit and all he was missing was his wife. Teva walked into his office with a double shot of Dusse for him. She sat the glass down in front of him then proceeded to give Gahd a massage in between the soft kisses she planted on his neck.

"Thank you, baby," Gahd said as he leaned back into her embrace.

"How's everything looking?" Teva questioned.

"Perfect; I'm booked and busy. This weekend's grand opening party is going to be epic. I hope you have your dress ready and your things packed; we're leaving Friday morning. You gotta be on point for this shit," Gahd said with a sly grin.

"This weekend? I thought the grand opening was going to be in two weeks? That's the date right here on my calendar," Teva spat anxiously as she looked at the calendar app on her phone.

"I told you last week that there was a 90% chance it was going to be moved up pending the completion of the renovations and the RSVP's for the party and room bookings. What difference does it make?" Gahd replied with a scowl.

"I have a very important test that day that I can't miss. I'm going to have to miss the grand opening. I wanted to be there with you. I'm your woman and I'm supposed to show my face and let it be known," Teva replied in a defeated tone.

"Damn, baby, that's alright. I'll make sure you can get to the one in Miami. You just focus on school. That's far more important than some party," Gahd said with a serious face.

"Thanks babe, I love you," Teva said before kissing Gahd on the lips.

"Yeah, I gotta get back to work; let me know when dinner is ready," Gahd said dismissing her. Once Teva was out of the room he smiled slyly. He knew exactly what he was doing, he was going to ask Bria to go to L.A. with him.

Just as he was fantasizing about spending a few days on vacation with her, the phone chimed with a message from her.

Bria: *Hey baby, I miss you.*

Okera: *I miss you, too. Am I going to be able to see you tonight?*

Bria: *Absolutely! I'm waiting for you... I figured we'd get some take-out and then "Netflix and Chill" for the rest of the night. Sound good?*

Okera: *Gimme me an hour and I'll be there.*

Gahd smiled as he looked down at his phone. At the same time Teva walked in to let him know that dinner was ready.

"What's got you smiling from ear to ear?"

"Nothing; is dinner ready?" Gahd asked, changing the subject.

"Don't worry about the damn food; who are you in here talking to, O?" Teva spat with jealousy dripping from her words.

"You must've slipped and bumped your head while you were in the kitchen? Because I know you got more sense than to talk to me like I'm one of those lame ass niggas off the block," Gahd spat.

"I just wanna know who you're talking to. Tell me the truth!"

"I was talking to my friend, now is there anything else you'd like to know?" Gahd questioned with a frown.

"Let me see your phone; give it to me!" Teva shouted.

"Man, get the fuck out of my face. I pay this bill and yours, I'm a grown ass man, and I don't have to answer to anybody," Gahd said as he jumped to his feet and walked out of his office, locking the door behind him. He grabbed his wallet, keys and tucked his gun in his back before he started towards the door.

"Where are you going O?" Teva questioned while closely trailing behind him.

"I need to get some air. I'll be back later," Gahd said as he walked out and closed the door in her face. Teva's eyes began to water; it felt like she was losing her man and she needed to know what bitch was occupying his time. Quickly, Teva went to the locator app on her phone to find out just what O was up to.

"How the fuck is he outside if I just heard him pull off? I know I saw him with his phone in his hand," Teva said aloud as she walked over to the garage. The car he took off in wasn't parked in the garage, so she couldn't figure out how his phone got there. It sat on the seat of his Benz, but he had driven the Range Rover. She shook her head at the thought of Gahd being sneaky. He had never done anything like that before.

"A whole fucking year and now this nigga wants to play games with me? Muthafucka!" Teva shouted before going back into the house. She sparked up a blunt and leaned back in the chair that sat at her vanity; she was about to be on her worse behavior.

∼

"Hey baby, I've been missing you," Bria said as she wrapped her arms around Okera's neck. He sucked on her bottom lip while gripping her ass as he walked her backwards into the house. It was the type of greeting a boss nigga deserved.

"I guess you really missed me, huh shorty?" Okera asked with a sly grin.

"Of course, did you pick up our Chinese food?" Bria asked anxiously looking around for the bags.

"Oh shit, I forgot!" Okera replied.

"Damn, I'm hungry," Bria said with a pout as the doorbell began to chime. Bria looked over at Okera and shook her head. He had the food delivered instead. She grabbed the bags from the delivery man while Okera handed him the money and a tip.

"Yo hungry ass was about to cry," Okera joked.

"That's not funny. I've had a stressful day. I just wat to stuff my face and watch a few good movies, maybe get laid…" Bria grinned shyly. Okera eyed her seductively and thoughts of their first time played in his head. The past few days since had been intense… it was almost like teenage fever. All they could think about was one another and they wanted to spend every ounce of their free time together.

"I'm sorry, B. I'll make it up to you a little later. Oh yeah, I wanted to ask you something…"

"O…k, what's up?" Bria asked cautiously.

"Well, you already know I'm opening up a couple hotels with the first being in L.A."

"Yes, I remember..."

"The grand opening is this weekend and I wanted to know if you'd like to fly out with me Friday and we'll come back Monday?" Okera asked nervously. No woman had ever made him nervous, but Bria had something on him.

"This weekend... uh, well..." Bria started. They were in the middle of this craziness at work and leaving for four days didn't sound like a good idea. However, with the look that Okera had on his face, she would've felt horrible letting him down.

"Let me see if I can get a few days off and I'll let you know."

Bria walked into the kitchen to grab a couple plates, utensils, and Cokes for her and Okera. She grabbed her phone from the counter and shot Dobbs a quick text.

Bria: *Hey Dobby... I know my timing is terrible, but I've been invited to L.A. for a few days. Do you think that's possible?*

Dobbs: *... Is it with a guy?*

Bria: *Um, what does that have to do with anything?*

Dobbs: *Because if it is, you can definitely go. It's been over a year since I've seen you with anyone other than Bryce. What days will you need off?*

Bria: *I guess everyone is over me being single, huh? It's Friday and I'll be back Monday.*

Dobbs: *Yeah, you've been kind of difficult for the past few months. You're my god-daughter, but you really need some loving, release some of that tension.*

Bria: *That's my cue, I gotta go. Thanks!*

Dobbs: *Lol, bye.*

Bria laughed as she took the things back into the living room to rejoin Okera. He was busy searching through Netflix for something good to watch. When she appeared before him, his eyes lit up. She was so damn beautiful in her tiny shorts that showed off her curves. Her hair was pulled up into a bun allowing him full view of her pretty face and mesmerizing eyes.

"Good news, I'm free to go. Apparently, everyone at work has been rooting for me to get laid. So, I'm basically being pushed to go because I've been such a bitch at work," Bria said with a giggle. Okera shook his head then patted the couch next to him.

"Come on, let's eat."

Thug Alibi

Bria sat down and plated their food before the two began to eat and watch a laughter-filled comedy. Occasionally, her eyes would wander over to Okera's face and then his body. She was still in awe over him. *He's so damn fine!*

Ding Dong! Ding Dong!

"Who the hell is that?" Bria said aloud with an attitude. She was trying to enjoy her time with her man and the last thing she needed was some asshole to ruin it. Without asking who it was, she snatched open the door and then laughed when she realized it was Syria.

"Damn, did you forget you had a best friend?" Syria questioned as she pushed past Bria and into the living room.

"No, I didn't forget. I've just been busy lately," Bria said as her eyes shifted over to Okera.

"Ah shit, my bad, I didn't know you were finally having company," Syria said with a sly grin.

"Hey Sy, what's up? Babe, I'm going to run to the bathroom. You two can gossip about me while I'm gone," Okera said with a smile as he stood up and walked past her.

"Ain't nobody about to gossip about your black ass," Syria said with a roll of her eyes. The moment he walked up the stairs, she hurried over to Bria and pushed her down on the couch.

"Bitch, I need all the facts before he gets back."

Bria laughed and then looked at the stares before she spoke.

"Damn, you're nosy as hell. Sy, he got a bitch falling in love… his sex was no joke," Bria said as her eyes started to glaze over and drift back to the other night.

"Shit girl, you weren't lying; he done put it down on you. Do me a favor, don't move too fast. He seems like a good guy, but I don't want to see you hurt again. I mean, I'd hate to have to fuck that nigga and all his shit up over you," Syria said honestly.

"Sy…"

"What? You're the cop, I can do what I want. Anyway, I'm going to get out of here, so you can have part two of your sexcapades. I love you, see you later," Syria said as she hugged her friend and hurried out the door.

Okera took his time returning to Bria and his food; he didn't want to interrupt their girl time. He had unintentionally overheard Bria talking about the other night and the shit stroked his ego. He was more than ready to feast on her body again. She had that good pussy that would have a nigga spending all his money and his time.

"I guess you're done?"

"Yeah, she's gone. I'm all yours…" Bria said seductively as she walked over to Okera. He stood by the steps with his dick brick. He was ready to eat, but the food was not what he had in mind. Bria lifted on her toes and kissed him sucking on his bottom lip. He picked her up, wrapping her legs around his waist before he turned and walked back up the stairs with her.

In her bedroom, he laid her down on the bed and pulled her shorts and panties off. Soft kisses up her thighs led him straight to her pussy. He licked his lips before he was ready to dive in. As soon as the tip of his tongue touched her clit, his business phone began to ring. It was a burner flip phone and was only used when he needed to talk street business. He ignored the call and continued. Bria's hand gripped his head and the phone went off again.

"Shit! I gotta take this," Okera said as he lifted up from the bed and licked his lips.

"Holla at me."

"Bro, I need to holla at you. Twelve came over to the spot a few days ago talking crazy. I need to meet up with you," Koki said on the other end.

"Alright, I'll be there in a minute," Okera said before he ended the call.

"Babe, I'm sorry, but I gotta go. There's some drama going on at one of my clubs and I need to be there to get it under control. I'm sorry to leave you hanging like this, but I promise I'm going to make it up to you." Okera felt horrible about leaving her, but his money and his family came before any bitch.

"It's okay, I understand. Go handle that and I'll be waiting for you when you're done," Bria said half-heartedly; she wanted him to stay. He kissed her pussy once more and then her lips before he hurried out the house. As soon as the door closed, she squeezed a pillow between her legs.

"Ugh!" She belted with anger. She was horny.

∼

Gahd pulled up to Koki's condo and hurried inside, using his key. He found his brother sitting on the couch, puffing a blunt. There wasn't a lick of worry on his young handsome face. Gahd needed to know what was up.

"You're rather calm for a nigga that feels infiltrated by the law, what's up?"

"Nigga, you already know nothing puts fear in my heart. Some bitch came to the club the other day asking questions about the murders in the hood. I sent her ass booking, but lately, there's been this nigga riding around in a Challenger. I think he's one of those pig ass detectives. My men spotted him sitting outside of both clubs. I thought that shit couldn't be tied to us?" Koki questioned with a lifted brow as he puffed on his blunt.

"It can't. I found out that the muthafucka that was feeding fake information to the police about us, was killed. That lame ass nigga Carti offed his own man based on some he says, she says shit. We're good, so don't worry about that," Gahd replied while reaching out for the blunt.

"I can't wait until that nigga's dead. You should really let me put a bullet in that nigga," Koki said as he lifted up from the couch with his eyes fixed on the older version of himself.

"I told you this shit has to be done right; we'll get him. In the meantime, can you please not interrupt me while I'm trying to get some pussy," Gahd said as he held out the blunt to Koki.

"Hold on, nigga, you keep licking your lips… don't try to hand me that shit back after you've been eating pussy. I got another one." Gahd erupted with laughter before he shrugged his shoulders and continued to smoke.

Chapter Seven

"I'll take that one and those," Gahd said to the salesperson in the Gucci store. He was getting Teva a purse and matching shoes. He felt bad about leaving her hanging for the weekend, especially after sleeping with Bria. He needed to be sure that things with her were real before he relieved Teva of her girlfriend duties.

"Yes, sir. Will there be anything else for you… maybe something for you?" The thin white woman asked with a smile.

"No, that'll be it," Gahd replied. He didn't have time to waste. He was going to surprise Teva at school.

"Sure. That'll be $1926.52," the woman said as if it were a couple of dollars. Gahd swiped his black card and once the transaction was completed, he hurried out to his car. He sat the bag in the passenger's seat next to the bouquet of her favorite flowers; Forget Me Nots and gardenias. Gahd arrived at her school and pulled his Bentley coupe up in the front of the entrance of her building.

A few minutes later, Teva emerged with a group of girls, laughing and talking as they walked towards the parking lot. When she spotted him, her eyes lit up with joy. She thought she was losing her man; his behavior was becoming unusual. And as much as she wanted to write him off, she was giving him the benefit of doubt. Teva was chalking it up to working to move towards this new "white-collar" life.

"Baby, wh-what are you doing here?" Teva questioned with shock.

"I came to apologize… I know work has been having me in a mood lately and I haven't been spending as much time as I used to. I'm sorry. I want you to know that in the end, this all is going to pay off and we'll be able to spend as much time as we want together. This is for you," Gahd said as he handed her the pretty bouquet of flowers.

"Aww, baby this is so sweet. You know these are my favorites," Teva said with watery eyes as she smelled the flowers. The girls behind her crooned at the sight. Gahd held up the bags, allowing her to grab them. She was so thirsty that she had to see what it was. She pulled out the purse and shoes that matched the flowers perfectly.

"Let's go," Gahd commanded as he turned and held the door open for Teva.

"What about my car?"

"We'll get it later. We need to go if we're going to make our reservation," Gahd said as he closed the door behind Teva and joined her in the car.

A short time later, they pulled up to Calico's Prime Steak. It was Teva's favorite restaurant outside of the ones Gahd owned. They pulled into the valet stop and stepped out of the car. Gahd trailed Teva into the restaurant, watching her lil' booty bounce underneath the fitted silver dress she wore. She was sexy, but he couldn't get Bria out of his mind.

"Reservations for two, Ali," Gahd said in his deep voice. The fitted grey polo shirt and slacks made him look like a sophisticated thug. Teva looked over at him with so much love in her eyes that the hostess had to smile.

"You two are such a cute couple," the pretty petite Black girl said.

"Thank you," Teva said with a blush. She was on cloud nine.

Gahd grabbed her hand and interlocked his fingers before following the woman to their table. He pulled out the chair for Teva before he joined her at the table.

"I'll take your drink order and your waiter will be over shortly. What would you like?" The girl said with a smile.

"We'll have a bottle of your best wine and a couple bottles of Perrier, thank you," Gahd said with an innocent grin before the hostess walked off. Teva eyed him lustfully before she spoke. She was somewhat shocked by his actions.

"I gotta admit, I didn't think I'd ever see you do something like this for me again. I felt as if I was losing you, O. However, I'm happy that I'm still an important factor in your life, despite all that you have going on. I miss this…" Teva admitted. Her pretty brown eyes looked up at him and he began to feel a bit guilty.

"Anything for you, babe; you've been working so hard and you deserve some quality time with your man. Anyway, I felt bad about you not being able to come to the grand opening. I know you wanted so badly to be a part of it," Gahd admitted.

"It's okay, you have to secure the bag and I'm working to have my own, so we're good. You just make sure to keep me happy and you won't hear a peep from me," Teva said with a serious face. Gahd smiled a bit before it faded when the waiter walked up.

"Good afternoon, are you ready to order?" The young man said with a pleasant smile.

"Yeah, we'll have the grilled chicken with pilaf and the salad, thank you," Gahd said before handing the waiter both menus. They always got the chicken; it was their favorite. The smile on Gahd's face faded when his phone vibrated with a call from one of the event planners.

"Hey, Okera speaking. Yes, that's correct; I want the V.I.P area to be sectioned off. If you look at the RSVP list, you'll see that there are quite a few celebrities coming out. I don't want them worrying about being bombarded by fans, so it's important that it's completed. Thank you and I'll see you tomorrow," he said before he ended the call. It brought him back to reality; he was going to be

Thug Alibi

spending the weekend in L.A. with his new boo, and he didn't have to worry about Teva finding out.

"Bae is everything okay?" Teva questioned as she watched Gahd's face contort with different emotions.

"Oh, yeah, they were just wanting to confirm some of my wants for the party Saturday. When I leave in the morning, I have to swing by to make sure my shit is on point. I gotta impress those mufuckas out there. To attract wealth, I have to exert it in my facility... Fine linens, great food, excellent customer service... all that. Since the hotel was already rated high with so many reviewers, I kept all of the top staff members and gave them a raise."

"You should see your face every time you talk about the hotel; you're going to kill it babe. I know you will," Teva exclaimed with honesty. Everything he touched skyrocketed with success. That was one of the reasons Teva wanted to stay around. She knew her career would take off using the weight of her man's name. He knew a lot of people and there was nothing or no one he couldn't touch... he was Gahd.

"Here you are," the waiter said as he sat the food down in front of them. "Enjoy your meal."

The couple chatted while enjoying their meal. It was just like the old times before Bria came into the picture. Gahd stared into her eyes then laid out his rules for the weekend.

"Look, I know I'll be all the way in L.A., but I don't wanna hear shit about you out here doing nothing with nobody. I don't want those lil' hoes in my house; they keep up too much bullshit. And last, but not least, stay your ass out of trouble; I'd hate to have to come back and fuck you before I put your ass out," Gahd said. Teva knew he was serious, but she wanted to test the waters.

"I told Passion and Mela they could come over to spend the weekend with me. They can't come?" Teva asked with a lifted brow.

"T, don't play with me. You know I'll fuck you up if you have those hoes in my house. Those lame ass niggas they fuck with will have our place looking like we're moving. They're not your friends; they're waiting for your first slip-up to move in on me, my money and my dick," Gahd said honestly. He hadn't told Teva, but her best friend Passion tried to throw the pussy at him on several different occasions. To avoid the bitch denying it and blaming it on him, he kept it to himself and forced Teva to keep her friends out of his space.

"I'm just playing, damn! I got it, babe, can we go now?" Teva asked with a chuckle.

Gahd stood up from the table and tossed $200 on the table before walking around to pull Teva's chair out. She stood up and fixed her dress after tossing her purse on her shoulder, and then interlocked her fingers with Gahd's. They walked over to the valet port and talked a bit before the car pulled up. Once they were situated, the pair started towards Teva's school.

"Where we going now? Get a lil' fuck session started?" Teva said with a lick of her lips.

"Nah, I gotta drop you off to your car and make a run. I need to make sure everything is airtight before I leave these muthafuckas in charge of my shit," Gahd said with his nostrils flared.

"You'll only be gone for one whole day. I'm sure they can manage that without you," Teva said with a shake of her head. Little did she know, Gahd was planning to spend a few days with Bria in L.A.

"Yeah, better safe than sorry. I'll see you at home later," Gahd said as he pulled up next to Teva's car. She leaned over and planted a passionate kiss on his lips before grabbing her bags and rushing out to her car. He watched her as she switched over to her car and pulled off.

Gahd took off in the opposite direction, making his way to his headquarters. He was meeting with his workers and giving clear instructions for the plans while he was away. Carti's niggas were all over the place, pulling fuck-ups on a regular and the last thing Gahd needed was for his people to do the same dumb shit.

He walked inside the small building that looked like an office and spoke to Callie, the receptionist, before heading to his office to change. The building was the headquarters for all his operations. Gahd had real workers as well as street niggas, so he figured having an actual office building for customer service and marketing opera-

Thug Alibi

tions would be the perfect front for his hustle. A huge room located in the back of the building, lined with distortion devices and metal detectors was the meeting spot for the street shit.

Gahd pulled on a pair of blue jeans, a red and white Balenciaga shirt with red and white J's. His watch glistened in the sunlight that beamed in through the window casting a flash of light on the wall. He stood in the mirror, giving himself a once over before leaving the room. Bria was the next thing on his list and he had to look the part when he saw her. He needed to hit all the important points quickly, so he could make a mad dash to his woman.

"Wassup G, you're looking good… you going on a date?" Kiki, one of his block runners, said with a grin. She was short and thick as fuck with a pretty face, and everyone in the hood knew she had a crush on Gahd. He brushed her off because she worked for him and she was a beast when it came to that hustle game. She kept her blocks hemmed up, her underlings went hard for her and her bag never came up short. She was an asset to him, and Gahd knew that fucking her again would ruin it.

"Maybe, why do you care?" He asked slyly.

"You already know why I care," Kiki said with a bite of her bottom lip.

"If you cared, you would've left this shit alone like I asked, and you could've had whatever you wanted," Gahd replied with a lifted brow. He was feeling her at one point and when he found out the feelings he had for her were mutual, he asked Kiki to give the drug game up. She wasn't going, so he left it alone. However, on a drunken night after he and Teva got serious, he and Kiki hooked up at her house. Gahd was her designated driver, turned fuck buddy for the night. Since then, the two would flirt, but nothing more. And because of it, Kiki hated Teva and the feeling was reciprocated.

"Okay, everyone have a seat. I need to make an appointment, so I'll get to the matter at hand. You all know about the hotel opening this weekend, some of you are coming, but the rest of you… I want this shit to be business as usual. Stay on your toes and just because me, Zeke and Koki aren't around doesn't mean you can slack off. I will have mufuckas watching your moves, so if you feel like being on some slick shit, getting careless or have a hiss of snake shit in your heart, know that I will deal with you when I return. If you're in this room, you already know how I get down, don't try me," Gahd said, seriously, his demeanor had changed completely. When he spoke to his people, he had to rule with an iron fist and ensure that they knew he meant business.

"We got it, boss, plus we gotta impress you. When you and Zeke step down, Koki is going to need a right-hand that's been in this shit with you for a minute. Most of us are using this opportunity to show up and show out," Shocky said. He was another block runner that kept his crew on their toes.

"That's what I like to hear. Business as usual and stay the fuck out of the way. Y'all have a prosperous and safe weekend. Gahd bless," he said as he closed out the meeting. He and the crew parted after a bit of small talk and Gahd was ready to catch Bria leaving the precinct after work.

He parked next to her car then leaned up against his car as he waited for her. Ten minutes later, Bria emerged wearing a scowl and a "fuck you" attitude. Okera had never seen her like that before; she was always in a good mood. The closer she got, the more he could see that Bria was pissed off. Her eyes finally gazed up from the folder she held in her hand, and suddenly, a smile appeared on her face.

"Hey baby, what are you doing here?" Bria asked while looking around the parking lot nervously.

"I came to surprise you. I want to take you to dinner," Okera said with a sly grin.

"I don't have much of an appetite right now. My boss has been on my ass and there's nothing I can do about it. Maybe I should take a raincheck on our trip so that I can work on this case a bit more," Bria said honestly.

"Hell no, you need this trip. I want to take you away from all this bullshit. As a matter of fact, get in your car and follow me."

"O, where are we going?" Bria asked cautiously. She didn't know how Okera found out where she worked, but for the time being, she was going to play his little game.

Thug Alibi

"Just follow me," Okera replied before hopping in his car. He took off and just as she was told, Bria followed him. They drove for almost an hour before they pulled up to a private airport. She looked around with confusion as she stepped out of the car and walked over to Okera.

"What are we doing here?" Bria questioned suspiciously.

"You said that work has been wearing you out and you feel like there's nothing you can do here. So, I'm going to whisk you away. The jets all ready to go and so am I. Let's get on board," Okera said with a grin.

"But, but, I haven't even picked up my things and you told me we were leaving tomorrow. I don't even have clothes to wear," Bria fussed as she walked onto the plane.

"Here you go," the flight attendant said as she handed Bria a flute filled with chilled Ace.

"Thank you. What am I supposed to wear for four days?" Bria snapped with an attitude. Her anger towards work was beginning to spill over into her time with Okera. He turned away from the flight attendant he was speaking to and got close to Bria's face before he spoke.

"You're so beautiful, even when you're mad. So, I can't figure out what the fuss is about… From this point on, I don't want you to worry about anything; clothes, money, shoes, your hair… none of that shit is important right now. You could be barefoot with your hair all over your head and sleeping in a box and you'd still be beautiful. I know that work has gotten to you, but when you're with me that attitude shit won't fly. But, if all those things are really important and you really feel like we need to address that matter right now, here," Okera said as he whipped out his black card and sat it on the small table in front of her.

Bria's jaw practically hit the table as she laid eyes on the card and from the way he spoke to her. He had checked her so good that there were very few words she could say. She decided to put her big girl panties on and fix the mess she had caused. Bria could see how her complaining had gotten to Okera.

"Babe, I'm sorry. I promise not to fuss anymore, and I'll leave work at work when I'm with you. And… is this for real?" She asked as she held up the credit card. Okera gave her a look as if to say, "are you kidding me?"

"Yes, it's real. I told you that I would take care of you and I meant that. Now, sit back so that we can enjoy our dinner," Okera said with just as much attitude. His nostrils were flared out and his sexy bedroom eyes were filled with rage. He took a few deep breaths and then sat down next to her, pulling the small tray table closer to him.

"A fresh salad tossed in a light bacon ranch dressing. Enjoy!" The woman said as she sat down the food and walked off. Bria had never had anything like this done for her before; she was overjoyed. She looked over at Okera and finally realized that she had pissed him off. He didn't say anything to her as he sat and ate his salad. Bria ate her food and glanced out the window every once in a while to catch the clouds floating by.

"The main dish; shrimp and crawfish Etouffee over white rice, garlic bread and steamed broccoli. Once you have completed dinner, you can sit the trays in the cart over there. You'll have privacy for the remainder of the flight, however, if there is anything you need, don't hesitate to call. The blue button on the remote will alert us. Enjoy the rest of your flight." The attendant walked off and pulled the sliding door closed behind her.

Bria ate most of her food and watched as Okera picked with the rest of his after eating half of it. He still wasn't talking to her and, somehow, it seemed odd to her that he would revert to the silent treatment. By no means was Okera a childish person, but to keep from blowing up on her, he kept silent. Bothered by the entire mood, Bria stood up and grabbed the dishes then placed them in the cart as instructed before she returned to her seat. She pushed the small tables away and then got on her knees in front of Okera.

"Are you going to be quiet the entire weekend? I don't think I can handle not hearing your sexy voice or seeing those bedroom eyes staring at me," Bria said with a grin while looking up at him. Okera's eyed peered into her and made her nervous. He had this anger in his eyes that she wasn't used to.

Thug Alibi

"I'm about to watch this movie; you can sit down and join me," he said without answering her question.

Bria wasn't about to let his fine ass get away with this. She had to make it up to him. She pulled the rubber band from her hair and allowed her long tresses to hang down her back and over her right eye, giving her this sexy look. She quickly unbuttoned his pants and pulled his dick from his underwear. His thick, chocolate dick made her eyes light up like a kid in a candy store. She had to have it. Bria licked her lips before sucking the head of his dick into her wet mouth.

"Sss," Okera hissed as he watched Bria suck and slurp on his dick like a porn star. She had sucked every ounce of anger right out of him. He bit down on his bottom lip and his eyes had her in a zone as she watched him enjoying her. She bobbed, sucked and slurped on his dick until he could no longer hold onto the nut that was building in his loins.

"Fuck, I'm bout to cum!" Okera grunted before he shot his release into the back of her throat, and like a good girl Bria swallowed it down. She licked her lips then got up and sat back in her seat with a grin. He laid his head back on the seat and fell asleep from the head she gave and a short time later, Bria followed suit.

∽

"Hey Zeke, have you seen Gahd? He told me he had to meet with y'all and then he was going to meet with everybody to set things up for the weekend. He said he'd be home after that," Teva asked with a bit of worry as she talked to Zeke on the phone.

"Uh yeah… he must've had some more business to handle. I'll see if I can get in touch with him and I'll have him call you," Zeke replied half-sleep on the other end. He hung up the phone and rolled over to plant kisses on Syria's neck as she slept. He looked up at the clock and it was two in the morning. They'd gone asleep at nine to get up early and get all of their last runs done before their flight to L.A.

Zeke stood up from the bed with his dick swinging as he pressed send next to Gahd's name and made his way to the bathroom to piss. The loud sound of him peeing almost drowned out Gahd answering on the other end.

"Wassup bro, everything good?" Gahd replied on the other end. It was only midnight in Cali, but he and Bria had worn each other out.

"Yeah, you good?" Zeke whispered in the phone as he looked out to ensure Syria was still asleep.

"Why are you whispering and yeah, I'm good. You called to ask me that?" Gahd replied curiously while shaking his head. He had stepped out onto the balcony for a quick smoke and Zeke was about to blow his high before it had even set in.

"Nigga, your bitch called looking for you. I told her you had some more business and that I'd try to get in touch with you… Syria is next to me sleep and Teva's blowing my phone up looking for you. Did you forget that Bria was her best friend? Where the fuck are you anyway?" Zeke questioned.

"I'm in L.A. with Bria. She was stressing about work, so instead of going out for dinner, I decided to feed her on the jet ride over. It was a spur of the moment thing. Let me go ahead and call Teva's ass right quick; Bria is asleep," Gahd said lowly before ending the call with Zeke.

"Baby, you good in there?" Syria called out to Zeke from the bedroom.

"Yeah, that was O's crazy ass. Let's go back to sleep," he said as he rejoined her. He wasn't trying to get caught up in any of Gahd's bullshit. He was sure Bria didn't know anything about Teva and the last thing he needed was for Syria to be blaming him for not telling her about it.

∼

"Hello," Gahd said nonchalantly as he blew out a cloud of weed smoke.

Thug Alibi

"Baby, where are you? I was worried sick after I couldn't reach you and it's already two in the morning," Teva whined.

"I had to run to L.A. a little earlier than expected. We had some complications with some of the arrangements, but I got it all straightened out. I meant to call you; I'm sorry about that," Gahd lied to save face. He was already counting down the days until he ended his relationship with Teva. Bria was the one and there was no point in prolonging the inevitable.

"It's okay. I just wish you would have told me. I can go to sleep now that I know you're okay. I love you babe," Teva said sounding calm.

"Yeah, goodnight," Gahd said then ended the call. He ashed his blunt before going back inside to slip into the bed with Bria. He wrapped her up in his big arms and drifted off to sleep a few minutes later.

The next day was filled with running around; Okera and Bria needed to get clothes for the weekend and get over to the airport to link with his people. Zeke, Syria, as well as Koki and a few of their friends were flying in.

"You ready babe," Okera asked as he started towards the door.

"Yeah, thank goodness for the giftshop downstairs, I don't know how comfortable I would've felt putting clean pussy in dirty panties," Bria said with a shake of her head. Okera erupted with laughter as he observed the serious look on her face.

"Yo ass crazy, come on." They walked out of the penthouse suite into the elevator and took it down to the lobby. Okera had the car pick them up and take them to a few high end shopping areas, allowing him and Bria to shop for three hours straight before they went to the airport.

O eyed Bria thirstily as they stood at the baggage claim area awaiting the crews' arrival. Bria spotted Syria and ran over to her, practically picking her up with excitement. The guys looked on as they watched the two of them act as if it had been years since they last seen one another.

"Bitch, you just up and leave town without telling me? I rang your doorbell for five minutes yesterday looking for you," Syria fussed with her hand on her hip.

"That would be my fault," Okera said bashfully as he held up his hand before turning towards his boys.

"Z, wassup G. Koki, don't get in no shit out here," O said with a lifted brow. Bria turned around at the sound of a familiar name. It was him, the guy that she attempted to question at the club. How the hell does he know Okera?

"I'm not doing shit but getting pussy; that's it, that's all," Koki joked before the guys laughed.

"This nigga already got about five numbers before we left O'Hare. So, you gon introduce us to your new wife," Lux said with a sly grin. He was one of Gahd's high-ranking men; he ran the largest hood under his command and brought in crazy dough. Lux was twenty-five living like a retired boss, he had niggas willing to lay down their lives for him. He was the right hand Gahd had in mind for Koki when he took over.

"Oh yeah, since you'll be seeing more of her I guess I should introduce you. But, before I do that, I need to tell y'all that she does not know Gahd or any of the shit associated with that name. To her, I am Okera, a respected businessman and I wanna keep it that way," he admitted just above a whisper.

"Nigga, how the fuck are you going to do that?" Koki asked with a scowl.

"I'm about to leave this shit to you, so my time in this game is coming to an end and there's no need to even bring it up to her," Okera replied.

"Kino, that means shut the fuck up," Zeke said with a chuckle.

"Fuck you," Kino replied, he was Lux's best friend.

"Damn girl, who are all those fine ass niggas that came with y'all?" Bria asked suspiciously.

"Look, you're not about to interrogate me or anyone else on this trip. Anyway, they're Okera and Zeke's friends. Koki is O's little brother," Syria said as they stood staring at the men.

"Really? Well, we're being waved over, let's go," Bria said as she led the way over to her man.

Thug Alibi

"Babe, I wanted to introduce you to some of my friends, you already know Zeke; this is Koki, my little brother, and this is Lux and Kino. This is my girl, Xiibria or Bria," Okera said with a sly grin. It was the one time and one time only, he allowed his boys to assess his woman from head to toe. She was worth flaunting and it was also his way of saying, she was off limits.

Koki pulled him aside while everyone else continued out to the car.

"Bro, what do you really know about this chick? I mean she doesn't know about your real life, but she's the officer that came over to the club that day. Are you sure she doesn't know?"

"Of course, I'm sure. She has no knowledge of Gahd and his street life being associated with me. She knows who you are and that's it. That lil' nigga that led her to you is dead as fuck, so there's nothing to worry about. Plus, she's already too far in to bring the law in this shit," Okera admitted with a grin.

"Damn bruh, shorty really got you in your feelings, huh? That lil' pussy must be powerful? I ain't never seen you like this, not even over Teva," Koki said with a chuckle as he and his brother started walking towards the door.

"Shut up."

That night, the group headed to one of the popular clubs to party one time before the real turn-up the next night. Okera was wearing cream slim-fitting slacks and a blue blazer with a light blue shirt underneath. His blue shoes matched his blazer and the Ray Bans he wore added even more to his sexiness. As usual, his waves were making bitches seasick and Bria loved it.

Zeke and the rest of the guys were dressed similarly, leaving the jeans and t-shirt thug attire at home for the night. Syria was sporting a green body-con dress with matching accessories and red bottom heels. Her cute cut was styled to perfection and her body was sick. She captured the stares of both men and women in the club. Bria walked in after her wearing a cream two-piece skirt set. The top was an off-shoulder crop top that showed off her cleavage and her lil' six-pack abs. The skirt stopped just at her knees and fit like a glove over her curvy hips and fat ass; she was stunning. Syria had pinned her hair to one side and threw some big curls in it to add a dramatic effect.

"Goddamn! How y'all two find women like that?" Lux said with lustful eyes.

"Don't worry about all that, you just make sure you stay the fuck in your place, you understand?" Gahd gritted with a murderous glare.

"I got you G, I ain't on shit. Chill," Lux said with a laugh before Koki hit his arm and pointed at a table of fine bitches in the V.I.P section across from them.

"Aye, we'll be back," Koki said as he led the way to the women with Lux and Kino following closely behind.

"So, are you enjoying yourself?" Okera asked with his eyes wandering over Bria's body. The way he looked at her did something to her every time. She was spent and for some reason when she was with him, nothing else mattered.

"Yes, baby. I'm having a great time and I can't wait for the party tomorrow. The hotel is amazing, and I know you're going to be super successful," Bria crooned with a grin as she grabbed Okera's hand. They were staring at one another intensely until a voice interrupted their conversation.

"Wassup O," the man said before Okera jumped up and hugged the man.

"Bizzy, nigga what's good?" He replied with a big smile. Zeke jumped up and hugged him next.

"Shit, I heard you're having a grand opening for your hotel tomorrow night. I didn't get an invite and I'm feeling some type of way…"

"I've been trying to get in touch with you for two weeks, but "mums" been the word. What's been up with you?" Okera asked with a lifted brow. Bizzy signaled for the three of them to step aside to talk privately, leaving Syria and Bria at the table.

"Girl, I could stay out here forever," Bria said with a grin as she took a gulp of the Ace and chased it with a shot of Patron.

"You! Hell, I've already been looking at spots to open my salon for Hollywood's finest. Zeke said that he'd ride with me if I wanted

Thug Alibi

to make that move," Syria admitted before tossing back the shot of Patron.

"Damn, so you were just going to leave me without even getting my opinion? I thought we were better than that?" Bria said. She could feel the alcohol starting to take an effect over her.

"Hell no, you already know I had a resignation letter on standby for you, bitch, you were coming too," Syria said with a serious face causing both to laugh.

"Your ass is crazy, you were just gon' take me, huh?" Bria replied with a shake of her head, taking down another shot then chasing it with a sip of the Ace.

Before Syria could reply, Okera and company walked up and rejoined them. He nestled up next to Bria with his right arm around her waist. Zeke kissed Syria upon his return and Bizzy sat down at the table with his eyes trained on Bria. She didn't want to seem rude, but his stares were making her uncomfortable.

"Hey big brother," a cute light-skinned girl wearing a tight red dress said as she hugged Bizzy around the neck.

"Bianca, what the hell took y'all so long?" Bizzy questioned with a frown.

"You know how Ari and Mena are... slow. Hey Zeke, hey O," the girl said with a stare at Bria. She didn't know why everyone had to focus all their attention on her. Syria was just as beautiful and hanging on the arm of one of their friends. Bria really didn't care; she just wanted them to get the hell out of her face.

"Okera, how are you? It's been a while," the beautiful woman said with a bat of her eyes. She looked mixed with something, her hair was long and curly, and her eyes were blue. She was thick with a fat ass that made her black dress rise in the back. It was clear from the way her eyes lit up when she saw Okera that there was once something between them.

"Sup Ari," Okera said nonchalantly before drinking straight from the bottle of Dusse.

"Nothing much, how are you?"

"I'm good."

The vibe he put out made the girl pull back from doing too

much talking and it was clear that she was in her feelings when it came to him. Bria was a bit overwhelmed with all the new friends and the personalities surrounding her. She wasn't the one for hanging out, so it was a bit much to take in; she needed a breather.

"I need some fresh air; I'll be back," Bria said before standing up and heading out of the front door with Syria following.

"Cocky, what's wrong?" Syria questioned with concern.

"That pretty bitch is clearly someone he used to fuck with. I'm not used to being around my man's ex-bitch; it bothers the fuck out of me," Bria admitted jealously.

"Girl bye! Yes, your man is fine as hell and yes, he had a bad bitch by his side at one point, but the nigga is here with you tonight. Don't let the ex-bitch fuck it up between y'all then he'll be looking for the next bitch. Focus on what you have to offer him and that smile he's had on your face since we got here," Syria said honestly. Since Moses, everything in her relationship with O affected Bria more than it should have.

Just like clockwork, Bizzy's sister and her friends came outside to smoke weed from a vape pen. Although they were standing on the other side, they watched as Bria and Syria went out there.

"Girl, can you believe that nigga? He's gon sit in there all smug and shit as if he doesn't know me. Two months ago, he was fucking my brains out, but now he has his lil' model bitch and he can't speak?" Ari gritted with an attitude.

"Fuck O, he'll be back in your face before he leaves this weekend, believe that. Anyway, they can't be doing too much; doesn't he have a girl back home? That is not the girl that was on those pictures Bizzy showed me," Bianca said as she blew out the cloud of smoke. Their view of Bria and Syria was blocked by a crowd of guys standing outside smoking as well.

"Exactly, just because he's a boss doesn't mean he can have what he wants. He's lucky we don't feel like being on no bullshit tonight," Mena added with a roll of her eyes. She had the body of a model, skinny with not too much of anything.

"Facts!" Ari shouted before they started to laugh then retreat to the club.

"You see what the fuck I'm talking about?" Bria said after they listened to the girls' conversation.

"I see, now what you gon do about it?" Syria asked with a lifted brow.

They went back inside with Bria sitting in Okera's lap. She downed two shots of Patron and a glass of Ace before she started to twerk to the music that was playing. His dick was at attention as she put on for the crowd at the table. Koki and the guys who had decided to stay with the group of girls, watched as Bria wound her hips and popped her big ass.

"Goddamn B," Okera crooned as he grabbed her ass; he was focused. Syria shouted her on as she recorded the scene and the faces of her haters that sat across from her, rolling their eyes. She needed evidence because she was sure that as fucked up as Bria was, she would not remember it.

By the end of the night, Okera was carrying Bria out to the car and eventually to the bed. He knew exactly what she was doing at the club and honestly, it was cute. She didn't get loud and try to fight like Teva would. She kept it cute and the bitches hated her even more because of it. Once Bria was tucked away in bed, he skimmed through his phone to check for missed calls; there was a message from Teva.

Teva: *I miss you so much. I know you're probably whipping everyone into shape over there. Call me when you get a little free time, I love you G.*

He placed his hand on his head and shook it before he tossed the phone aside and went out on the balcony. He needed to smoke some good trees to help him gather his thoughts.

∽

"Bryce, what are you doing here?" Det. Tate asked as he wrapped up the case he and Reed had just solved.

"I'm trying to go over some notes, but I think Bria has everything locked up in her desk. Who the hell told her she could leave anyway," Bryce fussed as he leaned back in his chair.

"Word is her man took her on a weekend getaway and he's

P.A.I.D, something you ain't. How you work with that fine ass, SINGLE woman every day and not try to get with her?" Det. Reed said with a shake of his head.

"Unlike you two, I respect Bria and our partnership. I'm not trying to mess it up; you see what happened with her and Moses."

"Uh huh, that just means she won't give your ass the time of day. Anyway, we're going to get out of here and leave you to it," Det. Tate said before he and Reed walked out.

Bryce was trying to get to the files Bria had pointing to Carti. The description that woman gave that day did not fit the suspect he had in mind. He needed to keep Carti and his crew in the clear. He was getting paid top dollar to ensure they were good. It was after midnight and he was still at the precinct snooping around, so when Dobbs came in, it scared the fuck out him.

"Det. Bryce, what the hell are you doing?"

Chapter Eight

"Thank you all for coming out and celebrating the night with me. I hope you reserve a few nights on your way out. Drink up and have fun!" Okera said as he held the glass of champagne in the air. The ballroom of the hotel was packed with people littered in black and white. The attire for the for night was black tuxedos for the men and white dresses for the women.

He looked over at Bria with a smile; he was ready to throw in the towel and leave that hood shit alone. Her being a cop was the exact opposite of who he was. Teva wasn't happy about him switching it up, but once she felt like he would leave she decided to straighten up.

"Tonight, was a success," Bria said as she stared into his eyes, taking his mind off everything that plagued his mind.

"Yeah, it was. Have you been enjoying yourself this weekend?" Okera asked with sincerity.

"I have, and I can't say that I've missed work either. What does this mean for me?" Bria asked with a giggle.

"It means that you're ready to get serious with me. We can work towards taking our relationship to the next level. I'll take care of you, we'll have some babies and we'll live happily ever after," Okera said; he was putting on. All he could think about was getting Bria back upstairs to the penthouse and stretching her out. In L.A., he was just a regular businessman with a fine ass woman on his arm. However, he knew the minute he made it back to the Chi, it was back to that hood boss shit.

"Oh, is that what it means? Let's just start off with a nice night of pleasure…"

"And pain," O added with a bite of his bottom lip.

"Damn O, you weren't going to save a dance for me?" Ari asked with a sly grin. Bria had forgotten about them coming in with his friend, Bizzy.

"Nah shorty, I'm with my lady. Be respectful," he said with a snarl. Okera was no fool; he knew exactly what she was trying to do. He was in a good mood and didn't feel like getting crazy with Ari.

"Damn, I'm sure your bitch doesn't mind you dancing with your friend," Ari said with a slur; it was clear that she was tipsy.

"Man, shorty move the fuck around with that bullshit. Come on, babe, let's head upstairs," Okera said as Ari jumped back in his face, allowing Koki to pull Bria aside. He needed to know what her motives were with his brother.

"You may have my brother fooled but I ain't going. I know who you really are and I'm not going to let you pin some fake charges on my brother," Koki spat with venom.

"What?! What are you talking about? He knows I'm a cop and why would I pin charges on my man. He's been nothing but honest with me; he's a legit businessman and I'm not trying to fuck up everything he's worked so hard for," Bria admitted with confusion. She didn't know why Koki was saying those things about her.

Koki realized Bria had no idea about Gahd's real life. She only knew Okera, the hard-working entrepreneur. He quickly switched up his tune, but not before adding in a final warning.

"You better be damn sure that my brother is who you want to be with. He's serious about you, and if this shit between you two is only a joke or game to you, know that I will be on your ass… I don't give a damn how fine you are!" Koki spat before he walked off.

Just as he was walking away, Okera grabbed her arm and

Thug Alibi

pushed her towards the elevator. He was trying to prevent Bria from hearing the bullshit that Ari said about him. Bria allowed him to pull her towards the elevator while her eyes followed Koki out of sight. She didn't know whether to be upset because she was threatened or amazed by the love Koki had for his brother.

Once they were in the elevator and the doors were closed, Bria looked up at Okera with a lifted brow. Her facial expression was blank, and her mood was calm.

"Why did we run away? I know you used to fuck with that girl. I'm not stupid. I'm a grown ass woman, you don't have to hide your past. I'd be childish as fuck for getting mad about something that happened before me," Bria admitted.

Okera smiled a bit and shook his head after Bria's statement. It wasn't about hiding his past with other women from her; it was about the respect. He knew how it looked having a bitch get crazy with him in front of her. He considered Bria his woman whenever he wasn't around Teva. He wasn't happy about playing games with them, but it wasn't time to decide just yet.

"I don't ever want you to feel like I allowed someone to disrespect you. I know how these hoes are; they'll do anything to get under your skin. You good?" Okera asked with this innocent look as he looked down at Bria who was leaning her head on his arm.

"Yeah, babe, I'm good. That shit didn't bother me one bit. I'm a cop, so I know you have enough sense to know not to test me," Bria joked. Okera reached down and grabbed her ass while kissing her lips passionately.

As soon as the doors opened, he scooped her up in his arms and carried her out onto the balcony. Okera had something in mind for that space since the moment he and Bria got in that room. He walked up behind her and pushed her up against the tall glass that lined the balcony. He unzipped her dress in the back and slowly pushed it down from her shoulders.

"Ooh, that feels so good, baby," Bria crooned as his hands roamed her naked body. She thanked the heavens for the dress she wore; it prevented her from wearing underwear.

Her face was pressed against the cool glass as Okera's hands roamed her body. He kissed her neck, her shoulders and her back before dropping to his knees. Bria's eyes got big as Okera grabbed her right leg and propped it up on the small table next to them. After pushing her forward slightly, his long tongue slithered between her legs and lapped her pearl. Okera licked and sucked her clit before his tongue slipped between her cheeks.

"Fuck! Lick it baby," Bria cried out as Okera proceeded to eat her ass like groceries. His thumb fucked her tightness while he continued to feast. She was spent and fucking Okera was all she could think about.

O stood up and turned her around, allowing Bria to undress him quickly. She was hot and ready to pop. He pulled a Magnum from the pocket of his pants before tossing them aside and pulling on the condom. Bria wrapped her legs around his waist as he lifted her from the floor. The breeze of the night caressed their bodies. Okera slid his thick, long dick into her tightness and moaned softly.

"Damn B... pussy is so good," he crooned with pleasure.

His hips slow wind to the sounds of her wet pussy smacking and gripping on his dick. It echoed off the glass and caused O to revel in the moment. He was in a trance as he cupped his arms under her legs, throwing them into the cuffs of his arms. His hands gripped her waist, allowing him a firm handle as he pumped in and out of her pussy with no mercy. Deep penetration and rolls of O's hips had Bria shaking as she came with convulsions.

"GOD! I LOVE YOU!" Bria screamed.

Okera smiled as quickly as those words left her lips; he had her. As much as he wanted to say it back, he couldn't. O had never been in love; he'd cared a lot for a couple women and maybe even had love for them, but in love, never. The time he and Bria spent together had him nervous; she was the perfect girlfriend. However, she wasn't his girlfriend, Teva was...

"Fuck me!" Bria screamed bringing him back to the matter at hand.

"Ugh, I'm about to cum!" O shouted before he shook and laid his head on her shoulder with heavy pants. Bria closed her eyes tight as she thought about what she had said. She'd been feeling that way

Thug Alibi

about Okera for a few days, but she wasn't planning on telling him about it until he said it first. Bria wanted to kick herself for letting the cat out the bag.

"That was nice, you ready to go again?" O asked with a sly grin.

∽

Back in the Chi, Zeke reassumed his position in the hood. The crew had left Gahd and Bria behind in L.A. and it was time to get back to the paper. He was making runs to pick up the money from each of the blocks. Since it had been a couple days since the pickups had been done, he was doing it himself instead. Zeke didn't want to wait any longer to check the totals. He had to make sure niggas weren't slipping while the bosses were away. Upon making his stops, Zeke discovered a dark blue Challenger tailing him. He made it to his final spot and decided to make a move before getting out. Zeke picked up his phone to make a call.

"Hey, where you at?" He said into the phone.

"I'm on the block, working. Wassup G?" The man on the other end said.

"You see that Challenger parked in front of you? I need you to take a picture of his license plate number; he's so focused on me he won't see you with your phone. Send the pictures to Bo and tell him I need info on that stat. I'm about to come in through the front. Tell Shocky to have a car waiting for me in the back. I need to shake this clown ass nigga," Zeke said before he stepped out the car and headed into the house.

"Wassup Z, the car is waiting in the back for you. We got eyes on that muthafucka outside so you good!" Shocky said the minute Zeke got inside the house.

"I'll keep y'all posted but keep your eyes on that nigga outside. I hate the fucking police… always into some shit!" Zeke shouted as he walked out the back door and got into the black BMW waiting outside.

Zeke drove with Jeezy blasting as he puffed on a blunt of Kush. His mind was churning with thoughts of the police lurking and the next moves for him and Gahd. He was on a mission to get out the game ever since he and Syria got serious. Every time he looked into her eyes, he thought about all the niggas he'd killed and all the dirt he'd done coming back on her. The last thing he wanted was for her to lose everything behind his ass.

He pulled up to the office to drop the money off to the accountant. Steph oversaw washing the money and insuring all the numbers added up. She was sitting in her office mashing the keys of her fancy calculator when Zeke walked in.

"Hey Z! You got something for me?" She said with a smile. Her cute, round face was beat with natural toned make-up and her long ,curly hair was pulled up into a high ponytail. She was sporting a fitted peach dress with a blazer on top. Her skin was smooth and brown; she was beautiful.

"Sup Steph, here's the money from the pick-ups. How has your day been beautiful?" Zeke replied with a grin.

"It's been pretty good... You know I like leaving the office at 5pm; it kinda makes me feel like I have a normal job. It's cool, though, the pay and benefits are great!" Steph joked as she grabbed the briefcase and popped it open, revealing stacks of money. She looked up again to read the look on his face. She could tell something was bothering him.

"Yeah... well, I gotta get home. I'm tired," Zeke said as he turned towards the door.

"You okay?"

"Yeah, I'm good. Somebody was following me earlier and I need to find out who he was. I'm waiting on the intel from that shit, but I'm cool," Zeke said realizing he was wearing his thoughts on his face. He had to straighten up before he went home to Syria.

"Oh yeah, handle that... I miss you... us. I know you have a girl now, but I just wanted to tell you that," Steph said bashfully.

"I miss you, too. You know that you'll always hold a special place in my heart. You're the mother of my child," Zeke admitted with a smile before he kissed Steph on the lips.

"So, why haven't you brought her to meet your daughter?" Steph replied with a lifted brow.

Thug Alibi

"Zoe is ten now. I have to be absolutely sure about this before I bring my girl into her world." Steph nodded in agreement before she smiled. She knew that moving on was scary for Zeke, but his fuckups prevented them from being together. After the last time he cheated, she left for good but remained friends for the sake of their daughter. They were only kids when they had her.

"Well, I have work to do. I'll talk to you later," Steph said as she turned back to the stacks of money on her desk.

Zeke walked out of the building and continued to his car. As soon as he turned the key the phone rang. A smile crept on his face as he watched Bo's number pop on his screen.

"Wassup?" Zeke answered.

"That plate number you gave me… it was Detective Bryce Sims. He works homicide and he also works for Carti. Those two muthafuckas have been working to take down you and Gahd for the past month and they'll succeed if you don't take care of it," Bo said over the burners they spoke on.

"We have a plan for that nigga Carti and since his lil' pussy ass pig wants to be a part of this, we got something for him, too," Zeke gritted into the phone. He was tired of playing with Carti, but he was going along with Gahd's plan for taking him out. If it was up to Zeke, he would've had Carti's head floating in Lake Michigan a long time ago.

Zeke ended the call with a grin on his face. That little bit of information had brightened up his mood. He was ready to see his baby. He started towards Syria with the music blasting.

Doing 80 in a 60, fuck a ticket
Cuz I ain't had pussy in a minute
I'm on the way, aye

∼

Gahd pulled up to his house and his guards were posted up as if he'd never left. He couldn't stop smiling with heavy thoughts of Bria plaguing his mind. He'd spent the past four days wining and dining and making love to her. It was safe to say that he'd become hooked on her in a short amount of time. She had him feeling some type of way.

The minute Gahd pushed open the door to his house, there was dead silence. Teva was nowhere in sight. She'd been out of school for an hour and according to her, she was focusing all her time and attention on studying. He walked through the house after tossing his bags into his bedroom, checking to make sure there was no funny business with Teva.

He walked into the entertainment room and found her bookbag tossed aside with her folders neatly stacked next to it. To be certain he wasn't tripping, Gahd checked the schedule she gave him again.

"Yup, three classes today until one, it's 2 o'clock and the school is forty-five minutes away. Ain't no way in hell she came and left that fast." Gahd shook his head with a snarl before turning back towards his bedroom. She was adding fuel to the fire and he was ready to be rid of her.

An hour later, Gahd was sitting in his office going over the numbers from the grand opening weekend. He was cheesing from ear to ear at the success he'd had and was on top of the world. The sound of keys rattling interrupted the googly eyes he was giving his work. Teva walked past his office then quickly doubled back to run in and greet him.

"Hey baby, I've missed you so much! How was your trip, the grand opening?" She blushed while throwing her things on his desk.

"It was straight; the hotel was booked up for the entire weekend and so far, we're almost at capacity for the next ten days. How has school been?" Gahd asked with the memory of Teva's thing sitting aside.

"It's been tough. I had to take a test today… I aced it. Aren't you proud of me bae?" Teva replied with a grin.

"Uh huh… Where are your books… your bookbag?" Gahd replied irritated with her lies. He didn't bother congratulating her on her work; she was about to make him fuck her up.

"Oh, I left them in the car," Teva lied nonchalantly.

"So, you went to school today, took a test and left your bag in the

Thug Alibi

car?" Gahd questioned, making sure they both were aware of the answers she gave.

"Yeah, but I don't wanna talk about school... I've missed my man and I'm ready to spend some time with you." Teva looked around his office as Gahd continued to look down at the computer but watched her through his peripheral. She was nervous as hell.

"We'll get to that soon enough. So, what's been the move for the past four days? What you been on?" Gahd asked. Something didn't feel right.

"I went to the club a few times and hung out with the girls. Koki saw me with them," Teva added quickly. It didn't take him long to realize she'd been playing around.

"Yeah, alright. I'm hungry, can you make me something to eat?" Gahd asked, looking up into her eyes. His sexiness had her stumbling over her words as she fought to maintain her cool.

"Yeah, I got you baby," Teva said with a grin before leaving the room.

Gahd was never one to check behind a bitch, looking through her phone and the shit she did when he wasn't around. He wasn't that nigga, but he needed to do it this time because when he left her ass for Bria he wanted a clear conscious.

He quickly picked up her phone and punched in her lock code before scrolling through her messages. For two days straight, Teva texted back and forth with Carti. Gahd clenched his jaw and shook his head. She was entertaining his enemy. Every muthafucka in the hood knew that her move was a sign of total disrespect and that they both deserved to have their shit busted. But he had something for both of their asses.

As soon as she returned with the food, Gahd stood up from his desk and grabbed his keys.

"I gotta make a run. I'll be back later."

"Damn, you just got here! Where are you going?" Teva yelled at Gahd as he hurried out the door.

He didn't feel like playing with her anymore. He needed to get some insight on what the fuck had been going down while he was away. Gahd may have been ready to end things with Teva, but he still had feelings for her. She just wasn't the woman for him.

∞

"Baby, how long is this going to take?" A curvy woman, with long red weave whined. She stood at the foot of the bed in all of her naked glory, looking on at Koki.

"Gimme a few minutes," he replied with a lick of his lips.

"A few minutes?! Nah, we need about thirty; you'll get your turn, damn!" The cute, thick girl that sported a low fade with designs in her hair replied with attitude in between sucks. They were taking turns fucking and sucking on Koki with no regard. The doorbell sounded off, cutting into their freak session.

"Oh, my God, I ain't never getting my turn!" The red head shouted.

"Man, shut the fuck up and get in the bed! You too!" Koki shouted at both women as he pulled on a pair of basketball shorts and slipped his feet into the matching Nike slides. His waves were spinning while he flexed his dimples; the girls were ready to pounce. He made his way to the door, grabbing the pistol from the hallway console. He held it behind his back as he looked through the peephole.

"Shit, nigga I thought you were a mufucka looking to get their wig split," Koki said as he stepped back and allowed his big brother into the house.

"You weren't about to do shit, wassup with your lil' ass?" Gahd asked as he looked around the lush condo draped in red and white Italian leathers.

"Nigga, I was about to get into something, but you came in here interrupting me. Anyway, did you enjoy your lil' bae-cation with shorty? I can believe you're fucking around with twelve... I mean, she is thick and fine than a muthafucka, but damn bro. Can you really trust her?" Koki questioned with a lifted brow as he picked up a rolled blunt from his coffee table and sparked it.

"Yeah, I did enjoy it. Bria is the one; she's bad and isn't looking to take me for everything I have. I'm feeling her, and you know a nigga like me has never felt this way about a bitch. And as far as trusting her, she knows nothing about Gahd. I don't have a record and there's no reason for her to tie that name to Okera. And while we're talking about trust, what has Teva been up to while I was gone?" Gahd replied as he grabbed the blunt from Koki.

"That thirsty bitch was in the club with her thot ass friends, dressed and dancing like hoes. She really was cutting up while you were gone. Bro, this bitch was hanging on niggas and getting a lil' too friendly to be Gahd's woman," Koki admitted as he grabbed the blunt and took a few pulls before blowing out a cloud of smoke.

"I knew that bitch was dirty. She's been texting that nigga Carti, so now I gotta watch my moves around that hoe," Gahd admitted with a snarl.

"Nah, bruh what you need to do is cancel that bitch and let me put a bullet in her hoe ass head," Koki gritted.

It was no shock to Gahd that Koki wanted to take her out. He always felt like she was only fucking with his brother to get information to feed to Carti. You gotta understand, Teva ran with a group of bag chasing hoes that would do whatever to get paid. Loyalty was never a part of their vocabulary; he didn't give a fuck what Teva said.

"Look, I still care about shorty, so I can't be putting a bag on her head just yet. I'm going to watch her moves for now and I'll keep you posted," Gahd said as he stood up. His phone rang and instantly put a smile on his face.

"Hey beautiful," he answered.

"Hey baby... I was thinking about you and I had to call to tell you how much I enjoyed our trip. I've never done anything like that before, but I enjoyed myself," Bria crooned into the phone, clearly wearing a grin.

"I'm glad to hear that; there's plenty more of where that came from. It's only the beginning of what I have in store for you. Look, I gotta holla at my brother for a second. I'll call you as soon as I leave here. Alright baby," Gahd said with a smile before ending the call.

"She got your ass running around here like a teenage bitch in

KAY

love. You slippin' pimp," Koki said with a chuckle and a shake of his head.

Gahd fanned his hand at him before the sound of the two women moaning could be heard from the other room. Gahd couldn't fight his curiosity; he pushed past Koki and peeked his head around the corner before turning back to leave.

"Nigga, you're such a fucking hoe. I'll holla at your thot ass later," Gahd said with a chuckle before closing the door behind him.

Koki didn't know what his brother was talking about until he walked in to catch his bitches doing a "69." They were moaning, and juices were splashing everywhere. Koki smiled as he stepped out of his shorts and got in where he fit in.

∽

"Look, I need y'all niggas to be cool for a lil' bit. It's getting hot around here and this shit is starting to fuck with my paper. I know everybody in here likes living good and eating, so let's keep this shit intact. Y'all can't be out here wildin' over fuck shit... Don't get me wrong, if a nigga brings it to you, finish it; don't start the shit if you don't have to," Carti explained with grit.

It was honestly his actions that were bringing heat to his spots. His recklessness with Boo's murder put the spotlight right on him. The murder was done on his block and behind one of his traps. He was performing like a rookie and despite his disdain for Bryce's advice, he had to take it.

The group agreed to follow Carti's command before they parted ways, leaving him to the phone call that came in.

"Hey baby, how are you?" Carti crooned into the phone.

"I'm good, just thinking about you daddy. He's back and now I have to start sneaking to get to you... this should be fun," the woman whispered into the phone.

"Hell yeah, fuck that nigga. I told you I would take care of you. All you need to do is come home," Carti admitted wholeheartedly.

"I can't just up and leave. I still love him and I'm not sure if coming back to you is a good idea right now. You fucked me over,

Carti, and I need to know that shit won't happen again," she replied solemnly.

"Teva, I love you and I fucked up... I admit that. I promise I'm going to spend every day making it up to you; just gimme a chance," Carti pleaded.

"I gotta think about it," Teva replied.

"Well, you think about it. I gotta go over here to this family get-together so I don't have to hear my father's mouth. I'll talk to you later, baby," Carti said before ending the call.

A short time later, he was pulling up to a big house in the far south suburbs that sat on a quiet block. The driveway was spilling over with cars and the sound of kids playing in the backyard could be heard from the front. Carti adjusted the red baseball cap he wore over his dreads before dusting off his red Gucci shirt and blue jeans to ensure the ashes from the blunt were gone.

"Hey, how y'all doing?" Carti asked as he shook hands and gave hugs to his family members as he made his way into the house.

"Carti, we didn't think we'd see you today, but I'm glad you're here. Now, come over here and give your grandma a hug," the short, fair-skinned woman said. Her long hair hung to the middle of her back and made her look much younger than the grandmother of a grown man.

"It's about time you brought your yellow ass around your family. Your mama raised you to be just as bougie as she is," the older version of Carti said. He and his father both sported dreads with freckles and handsome faces.

"Wassup pops," Carti said as he shook his father's hand before he was pulled into a hug.

One of his aunts handed him a plate of ribs, potato salad, baked beans and corn on the cob. He was high with the munchies; Carti was about to kill that plate. As soon as he picked up a rib, a familiar voice interrupted.

"Hey grandma! Hey daddy, I'm sorry I'm late. Those crazy heifers at that shop seem to think I don't have a personal life. I really need a vacation."

"Hey baby, it's okay, you were over here all night helping to get things ready, so I guess I can let you slide for now," Grandma Lu said with a grin.

"Oh, she visits, huh?"

"Yeah, she makes time for her family," Carti's father said slyly.

"I guess her mama didn't raise her bougie like mine, huh? Wassup sis," Carti said with a grin.

"Don't speak to me. I still haven't forgiven you or your punk ass friends for what you did. Lame ass!"

"Syria, please let that go. Your brother was just trying to protect you," Grandma Lu pleaded.

"Whatever, I'm going outside to eat," Syria said with a roll of her eyes before she walked out of the patio door.

"Y'all two still acting like strangers in these streets?" Carti's aunt asked.

"Yeah, if she's not claiming me, I'm not claiming her. I'll always look out for her, but no one needs to know she's my sister. We have different mothers anyway," Carti said nonchalantly.

"Yeah, okay," his father said before taking a swig of his beer.

Truthfully, Carti was bothered by the relationship he had with Syria. He wanted to claim her and be a part of her life, especially since he found out she was fucking with Gahd's right hand man. He shook his head and continued to slaughter his plate before getting seconds.

"Damn, this food is good!"

Chapter Nine

Bryce combed through the files on his desk in search of the evidence he created against Gahd's people. He was sure he had it stacked with the rest of the evidence, but now it was missing.

"Damn!"

"Jones, my office, now!" Dobbs shouted from the crack in his door. Bryce knew he was looking for the files on the cases he and Bria were working on. Since she'd been out of the office, Bryce had been "working hard" to get them solved.

Bryce walked into the office with a bit of fear on his face as he looked over at his boss.

"Where's the damn files on the cases you've been working? I need to turn something in to the chief. You know the mayor is breathing down his neck about these murders, and in turn he's breathing down mine. Now, where's it?" Dobbs spat with anger.

"I have to talk to this last witness today and I'm done. Just give me until tomorrow morning," Bryce pleaded.

"Tomorrow or I'm going to have your ass. Get out of my office!" Dobbs shouted, dismissing Bryce before picking up his phone to make a call.

"Damn, did you get fired?" Det. Tate asked.

"Mind your fuckin' business… then maybe your black ass can get some cases solved. Muthafucka," Bryce said, whispering the last part as he walked off. He needed to find those papers to put Gahd's name in the mix and get his on the suspect list. Bryce walked over to Bria's desk and searched her folders for the fake files.

"Bingo!" He hurriedly put the papers back in place after getting what he needed. Bryce slid the paper into his folder then left; he had to make the witness interview seem real. He came back two hours later with a grin as he handed the files over to Dobbs.

"So, when are we going to start bringing these suspects in for questioning?" He asked waiting for Dobbs' thoughts. A smile crept on his face before he replied to Bryce.

"I'm going to let the chief know we have a few suspects in mind and then we'll rally up the task force to bring them in. We can't rush into this; we have to take our time if we're going to get these muthafuckas and make it stick," Dobbs said with a stern look.

"No problem, I'm ready whenever you are boss. I'll be at my desk if you need me," Bryce said with a look of satisfaction. He'd finally completed his half of the mission, now, all he had to do was sit back and collect his pay from Carti.

∼

"Girl, that nigga came back looking like a whole snack. I tried to suck the skin off that dick. I've missed him, and he hasn't even fucked me yet," Teva confessed to her friends as they sat on the block puffing a blunt as they leaned up against a gate.

"He probably heard about you being extra friendly with Carti… You need to chill before your black ass gets caught. Every fool in the hood knows Gahd ain't one to be played with; your ass better be careful," Passion said with a roll of her eyes. She was waiting on Teva to fuck up, so she could try her luck.

"Whatever, I'm not doing nothing. I'm just talking to an old friend, that's it. Anyway, Gahd is my baby and I'm not trying to fuck with anyone else, especially not Carti. He played the fuck out of me

Thug Alibi

and I can't risk playing his fool again," Teva admitted. A piece of her heart still belonged to Carti, but she wasn't ready to backtrack.

"I got these Gucci shoes, size 8... $30," a skinny lady said as she walked up to Teva and Passion. The woman was missing her top two front teeth and was dressed in a pair of dirty Air Force 1's. The cut-up shorts she wore help to show off her ashy, scarred legs.

"Tita, get your crackhead ass away from here! Don't nobody want those dingy ass shoes," one of the block boys spat as he shooed the woman away. Teva shook her head before her attention was grabbed by the tall nigga standing before her. He chopped it up with the corner boys and the grin on his face made her blush. Carti had a way of doing that to her.

"Ah shit here comes trouble," Passion said with a giggle as Carti walked their way.

"Wassup shorty," Carti said with a grin as he looked at Teva from the feet up. Her toes were painted an innocent pink, while the heather grey bodycon dressed hugged her curves. Her long weave hung over her shoulders away from her pretty face and he was ready to take things further.

"Hey Carti."

"You came over here to see me? When you gon' stop playing and fuck with a nigga?"

Zero looked on with a shake of his head, he'd been warning his best friend about going back with Teva. The bitch had Carti fucked up behind her after their split and even though he cheated on her, he was in love with her.

"Hmm, how about we get out of here right now? I'm ready to go," Teva said with bloodshot eyes; she was high as hell.

"Let's go," Carti said as he led her to his car and took off. Thirty minutes later, they were pulling up to fancy hotel in the suburbs.

"What are we doing here?" Teva asked playing coy. She knew exactly what was about to go down. Carti gave her a look that said shut your mouth and get ready to fuck. Teva was high and in her feelings, and Gahd putting her on the backburner didn't help. It had been well over a couple weeks since she'd had some dick and she was horny.

"I'll be right back," Carti said as he stepped out of the car and made his way into the lobby of the hotel. He was gone for ten minutes before Teva's phone rang.

"Aye, take the keys out, lock the car and come inside. I'm in room 420, I'm waiting on you," Carti said then ended the call. Teva nervously did as she was told. She was about to do something she swore she'd never do again… fuck with Carti.

She made her way up to the room then pushed the already cracked door open, locking it behind her. Carti had run a bubble bath in the huge jetted tub and was sitting inside waiting for her. Teva stood there staring at him. She was too damn nervous to move.

"You gon join a nigga or what? I got all this for you and we can't let it go to waste," Carti said with a sly grin. Teva smiled then began to undress. She knew that if Gahd found out, she and Carti would be as good as dead.

"This shit has to stay between you and I. Gahd will kill me!" Teva said with worry on her face. Her panties were the last thing to hit the floor before she stepped into the tub with Carti. Immediately, his hands began to roam her body, groping and massaging her breasts.

"I got you shorty, this will be our secret until you come back home. That nigga can't do you like I did." Teva rolled her eyes with thoughts of Gahd making love to her threatening to make her run out the door. Carti was good, but he was no Gahd.

Teva climbed into Carti's lap, straddling him as she slid down on his dick. A soft moan escaped her lips as she bounced with the water splashing up on her ass. Carti's eyes rolled around in his head with enjoyment. He gripped and smacked her ass, guiding her movements.

"Fuck! I miss this good shit," Carti admitted with a moan.

Teva was too busy enjoying the first piece of dick she'd had in weeks to pay attention to what Carti was saying. He held on tightly as he pumped faster, matching her rhythm. It wasn't long before the two of them were panting heavy and shaking with climaxes. The pair climbed out the tub and took a quick shower before retreating to the bedroom.

Thug Alibi

"Damn, I can get used to this… tell me you didn't miss that," Carti said feeling full of himself.

"Yeah, I can't lie I did, but we can't keep doing this. This was a one-time thing, I'm sorry," Teva admitted as she nestled up to Carti while looking into his eyes.

"So, you mean to tell me that you came all the way over here with me, just to fuck once and tell me how you're scared of that bitch ass nigga?" Carti gritted as he sat up in the bed.

"I wanted to be here with you and yes, I do miss you. But, I'm scared of what Gahd may do. You two are enemies and me going back to you is only going to make things crazier," Teva exclaimed.

"Fuck him! Leave that nigga and come back home to me. I won't let shit happen to you… that nigga won't touch you. Also… I need you to tell me what his plans are, just give me something, shorty," Carti said seriously.

"What?! That's why you were so thirsty to get me in bed… just to get info out of me? I knew you were full of shit!" Teva shouted with an attitude. She jumped up from the bed then rushed over to grab her clothes.

"T, it's not like that. My feelings for you are real. I just need help getting this nigga out the way. He's blocking my fucking money and I can't have that. I know you're all in love with that nigga, but trust me, there's plenty of bitches spending time with your man. That nigga doesn't want you. I do and I'm willing to do whatever to keep you. You just have to help me out, here," Carti said solemnly.

Despite what Zero had been spitting in his ear, Carti was determined to get Teva back. He was over being mad at her for leaving him for Gahd. She was his first real love and he knew her. Teva made Carti feel comfortable, but she was always a distraction when it came to business for him. When she left him, Carti went hard and the team's money started to grow.

"Prove it then," Teva said. She was fully dressed and ready to go.

"You see this…" Carti said as he pointed to the tattoo on the front of his neck.

"It's forever, my love for you is forever. Here, this will be a start,"

Carti said as he reached over to the Gucci bag that sat next to the bed, stuffed with blocks of cash and a pistol. He grabbed a stack of money that was double wrapped with rubber bands and tossed it over to her. Teva smiled at the money before flopping down on the bed next to Carti.

"Okay."

~

Gahd sat in his office scrolling through Teva's phone. He'd added the app that would allow him to view her phone without actually touching it. A text popped up from Carti and suddenly Gahd was interested.

Carti: *Last night was just like I remembered. The tight wet wet had a nigga remembering why he fell in love with you. When are we going to link again?*

Gahd clenched his jaw then tossed his phone on the desk. He couldn't believe his bitch was out there fucking his enemy. He was seeing red and all he wanted to do was see Teva, so he could put her head in the wall. The app chimed again, but this time it was Teva responding.

Teva: *I had fun and I'm glad you enjoyed yourself. I'm heading home to him right now, but I'll let you know baby.*

Ten minutes later, Teva was walking in. Gahd sat in the entertainment room watching a movie while puffing on a blunt. The thick cloud of smoke floated over his head while murderous thoughts roamed his mind. It was crazy because he was over Teva. It was the fact that the one nigga he wanted to kill was fucking her, and that got under his skin.

"Hey baby," Teva said as she walked in with bags of food from Walmart.

"Sup shorty. What's been up?" Gahd asked nonchalantly.

"Nothing much, I got the food for dinner later. How has your day been? I see you haven't gone back to your suit and ties just yet," Teva questioned. When Gahd did his corporate work, he'd don a suit, but since he'd been back from L.A, he'd been dressing casually.

"Tomorrow. I gotta go spend time with my shorty and she like that thug shit," Gahd said as he stood up and started towards the door.

"What?" Teva shouted with shock.

"I'll be back later. I'll give you a little time to talk to whatever niggas you're spending time with," Gahd said before leaving. He was going to meet Bria for lunch; it was their first real date since they'd been back from L.A. They spent the past couple weeks laying up and fucking whenever she wasn't working.

He pulled up to La Parreira and climbed out his Bentley, tossing the keys to the valet. It was his favorite upscale Mexican spot and he wanted Bria to experience it. He walked inside and quickly spotted the love of his life waiting for him at the table. The yellow dress she wore left little to his imagination and the floral printed Louboutin's made her thick, long legs go on forever.

"Damn babe, you look good," Okera said as he assumed his role.

"Thank you, baby, you look nice as well. It feels good to be out in the world again. You know laying up, eating, fucking, and sleeping was terrible for my figure," Bria joked as she rubbed her belly. Her abs were still on point, but since she'd been fucking O on a regular, she'd gotten thicker. Her ass was fatter, and her breasts were supple; it reminded her of when her aunties talked about her cousins fucking when they were teenagers.

"Yeah, that good dick will have your hips spreading all over the place. You look good, babe," Okera admitted with a grin.

"Well, I guess I have you to thank for my wide ass hips now."

Okera laughed at Bria before the waiter walked over and took their order. He was ready to move her in with him, but he had to evict Teva first and tonight was the night. It was the only time he'd been with Bria and couldn't get Teva off his mind.

"What's the plan for tonight?" Bria asked thirstily She was ready to hop in bed with Okera as usual. They'd been going at it several times a day, every day since that first day in L.A.

"I have to handle some business after this, then I'll be over to spend the night with you. Is that alright, baby?" Okera questioned.

"Yeah, that's cool. As long as you're coming home to me later, I'm fine. I know you have money to make and people to boss around, so I won't trip on you," Bria admitted. O nodded his head in agreement before tossing a bite of his food into his mouth.

Once their dinner was done, he walked Xiibria out to her car and kissed her goodnight. After watching her take off, he hurried to his car. He couldn't take one more second of being tied to that bitch at home. The thought of her rolling around with Carti made his blood boil and to keep from hurting her he had to leave her alone. He was finally ready.

As soon as he made it home, Teva rushed him at the door with anger. What he said when he left still had her in her feelings. She was ready to flip when Gahd got back; her eyes were bloodshot from drinking and crying. She had lost it when she started to hit Gahd in his chest.

"You're cheating on me now, I can't believe you. Why are you doing this to me Okera? I love you and you got me out here looking crazy," Teva slurred with tears streaming down her face.

"Shorty, are you fucking crazy? Take your hands off me before I bust your shit," Gahd gritted as he backed away from Teva. "You're out here texting and sweet talking my enemy and you didn't think I would find out. Bitch, you fucked that nigga and came home to me. Smiling in my face like shit was sweet, so don't come crying to me about what I do in these streets."

"I LOVE YOU! That shit I did was a mistake, I'm sorry Gahd," Teva cried as she grabbed on Gahd. Without saying another word, he grabbed her by her throat and pushed her off him.

"We're done. Pack up all your shit; you can keep everything I bought you, but you have to get the fuck out," Gahd roared. Teva knew he wasn't playing; he had never laid a finger on her but when he grabbed her she knew that was her cue.

She rushed into the bedroom and grabbed all her clothes, shoes, bags and accessories and packed them up in the suitcases she brought her shit in. Gahd instructed one of his men to use his truck to take all her shit wherever she wanted to go. He had washed his hands of her and there was no coming back.

Thug Alibi

Teva picked up her phone and called her best friend Passion.

"Hello, he put me out... he found out about Carti and he put me out," Teva wept.

"I told your ass... come on over, you can sleep in the guest bedroom until you find a place," Passion replied before ending the call.

Teva drove with her music blaring; her heart was broken, and she was enraged. She couldn't believe she allowed herself to fuck up her situation. Gahd never told her that he loved her, but he always treated her like a queen and to know that that shit was over made her mad at him and herself.

"He's going to pay for leaving me... that shit was supposed to be forever," Teva said as she wiped the tears that clouded her eyes and pulled a half-smoked blunt from her center console.

You gon' gain the whole world
But is it worth the girl that you're losing?
Be careful with me
It's not a threat, it's a warning be careful with me

∼

Bria decided to stop by Syria's place until Okera was ready to come back to her place. It had been a few days since she'd spoken to her and she couldn't wait to update her on her new relationship with O. For the first time in over a year, she was happy, and she couldn't wait to talk about it. She pressed the doorbell next to Syria's door and awaited her answer.

"Hey boo!" She shouted as she pulled the door open. Bria knew she'd already spotted her on the security camera before she opened the door.

"Hey, I've missed you, so I thought I'd surprise you with my presence," Bria replied.

"Uh huh, get your ass in here. I was just about to have me a lil' sippy sip, do you care to join me?"

"Go ahead and get me a glass," Bria said with a roll of her eyes; she knew what was coming next.

"Good, because you were going to get one anyway. So, how have things been with your new boo?" Syria questioned.

"Things have been great! The trip to L.A. was everything, the entire experience was new to me and I can't lie I can get used to living that life. I mean, I knew he had money, but he had a bitch feeling like a movie star. Aside from all that, the way he treats me is different from any other nigga I've been with. He can actually hold an intelligent conversation, he's fine as hell and his sex is bomb as fuck," Bria admitted with lust-filled eyes.

"Eww, do you need some time to yourself. That nigga has really gotten to you. You're acting like you're in love..." Syria said awaiting Bria's answer.

"Well..."

"Aw hell nah, girl you just met this nigga!"

"You love Zeke!" Bria replied to take the heat off her.

"Yeah, but he and I have years of history, you don't know Okera like that," Syria admitted. She couldn't get the conversation she overhead at the cookout out of her mind. She hadn't had the chance to talk to Bria about it; it was never the right time.

"Yeah, I'm at my grandmother's house, we're having a family barbecue. Once I leave here it's back to business. I told you I'm going to find another way to get to Gahd's bitch ass. Teva lives with that nigga so if I can get her to switch up in the process of winning her back, I'm in there. I told her I don't give a fuck about the business this nigga has as Okera, it's when he's in these streets being Gahd that I'm worried about," Carti said into the phone while Syria listened from the other side of the cracked door.

"Could this be the same person?" She questioned as she walked away. She needed to talk to Bria.

"Sy, I'm good, I trust that I'm making the right decision with him," Bria said with a reassuring smile.

"Do you know what he does for a living?"

"Yeah, he works with Zeke. He owns several businesses... I mean you did go to the hotel grand opening the other night. He's an entrepreneur and a good guy, why are you asking?" Bria questioned suspiciously.

"Look, maybe he's not who you think he is," Syria said with worry.

"Why would you say that?"

"Just be careful, Cocky. I can tell you're falling hard for him and I don't wanna see you hurt. I love you and I'm just looking out for you," Syria said solemnly.

"I'll be okay, don't worry," Bria replied as she stood up and hugged her best friend, her sister. A few seconds later, her phone chimed with a message.

Okera: *I'll be there in fifteen.*

Bria: *I'll see you then, baby.*

"Alright, I have to go. I'll call you in the morning and stop worrying," Bria said before hugging Syria again and ducking out the door.

Chapter Ten

Xiibria sat at her desk working a new case they'd picked up earlier that day. She was beyond ready to get home and spend time with O. It had been about two-and-a-half weeks since the trip to L.A. and they were hot and heavy. She had finally started spending time with him at his place. Hell, she was beginning to think he had a woman at home after the third date and there was no mention of going back to his place.

"Man, this day is just lingering on. We already have the suspect in custody for this new case and there's nothing to do," Bryce fussed before he decided to use his time to flirt and snoop on Bria.

"So, B, what's been up with this new boo of yours? Is this thing serious or are you two just fucking?" Bryce asked causing Bria to instantly frown up with displeasure.

"Can you get out of my business? Dang! Don't worry about what the fuck me and my man be doing… tend to your happy meal hoes," Bria spat causing their co-workers to chuckle.

"Yeah, whatever."

Bria was about to say something else smart when a woman who seemed lost wandered into their department. She didn't know who the woman was, but she seemed lost and Bria felt it was her job to help.

"Hi, can I help you with anything?" Bria questioned with sincerity.

"Yes, I have some information on the murders that have been occurring... I know who the suspects are, and I can give a full description as well as evidence," the young woman said nervously.

"No problem, we can help with that. What's your name?" Bria replied.

"It's Callie... I—" The woman started before her eyes shifted over to Bryce who was walking up to them. Terror filled her eyes and without speaking she quickly turned and ran away. Bria hurried to catch up to her, stopping her just outside of their department on the stairs.

"Ma'am, I thought you had some information for us?" Bria questioned suspiciously.

"That man... is he your partner?" The woman asked with fear in her eyes.

"Yes, he is... why?"

"I don't wanna talk to him. I'll talk to you, but I won't talk to him," Callie said with tears streaming down her face.

"Okay, it's okay, you can talk to me. You can trust me... talk to me," Bria said solemnly. She didn't know what it was about Bryce that had the young woman so frightened, but she was going to get to the bottom of it.

"Your partner... he was there. When the murders happened, he was there with them. He's working with them and he knows who's behind all of this. Please be careful around him; he's a fucking snake. He killed my cousin Brisco and I saw him with my own two eyes. That muthafucka!" Callie spat with anger.

Bria stomach turned at the sound of Bryce's name being tied to Brisco's murder. His bracelet was there at the crime scene, and he was anxious as hell to give the case over to Curt and Reed. As much as she hated to admit it, Bryce had been acting weird lately and especially when it came to the cases they were working on. It was as if he was trying to avoid solving them. Callie's answers only solidified what Bria was already thinking.

"Look, I'm going to make sure he goes down for what he did, that's a promise. I'm sorry for your loss. Here's my card, call me if you need anything or if you have any more information," Bria said while rubbing Callie's back.

"Thank you and be careful," Callie said as she turned to walk away.

"Wait, do you have a number I can reach you at to keep you updated?"

"Here's my number," Callie said before rushing down the stairs and out the door.

Bria swallowed deep before she returned to her desk. Bryce stared at her with confusion as she fought to avoid eye contact. She tucked the phone number in the front pocket of her jeans and kept quiet about what she and Callie had spoken about.

"You good B?" Bryce asked with a lifted brow as he glanced over from his desk.

"Yeah, I'm good."

"Wassup lil' bro," Gahd said as he shook up with Koki and walked into his condo.

"Ain't shit. Over here trying to get this lil' bitch to get her mind right," Koki replied with attitude.

"I don't give a fuck what you talkin' bout; you're not about to sit here and tell me that you didn't have another bitch over here. Who the fuck was she?" The girl shouted. She was about 5'7 with smooth peanut butter skin. Her hair was braided and pinned up into a bun, showing off her pretty face. She had a slim waist and a fat ass like a stripper.

"Shorty, I told you that was just my friend, why are you tripping?" Koki exclaimed.

"Do you need me to come back at another time?" Gahd asked with a grin. He knew Koki's ass was pump-faking, acting like he didn't have some bitch tying him down.

"Nah bro, you good. She's about to take her ass in the other room... she needs to go lay her punk ass down."

"I don't need to do shit. You need to tell your brother to leave. I'm sorry Gahd, but his ass ain't getting away with this shit," the girl said with sass.

"You got it, Tink, I'm about to gon get out of here. Let me just holla at him for a few minutes; it's about business," Gahd replied with a serious face and just like that, Tink backed off and retreated to the bedroom.

"Damn nigga, what makes you so special that this bitch follows your command with no argument?" Koki questioned in a matter of fact tone.

"Muthafucka, I'm Gahd, nuff said. Now, let me holla at you about what's been going on. Remember how Zeke said he was being followed? Well, I had Callie make a stop at homicide for me. She talked to Officer Xiibria Sams."

"What, your girl?!" Koki shouted.

"Yeah, she basically put that bitch ass officer at the scene of most of the murders, including Brisco's. Niggas saw him do that one. Callie said that Bria was eating that shit up and that she's going to be on his head now. I had to throw this shit off us... Oh yeah, I got rid of that bitch Teva. Nigga, she was fucking Carti and the hoe really thought I wouldn't find out," Gahd said with a shake of his head.

"Man, I told you to let me cancel that bitch. I bet she's over there right now running her mouth to that nigga about your business. That's alright, I'ma catch that hoe slippin'," Koki said with a clenched jaw. And just like that, Teva's fate was sealed. Gahd didn't deny him the right, so he was going to carry out his wish sooner or later.

"That's been three minutes, times up," Tink shouted from the other room causing Gahd to erupt with laughter.

"Alright bro, I'm out. I'll holla at you later if you can have phone calls."

"Ha ha ha, fuck you! Bye!" Koki teased before slamming the

door and locking it behind Gahd. You could hear Tink fussing at him from the other side of the door.

"Damn, she gon' beat his ass," Gahd said aloud before he retreated to his car and took off.

An hour later, Gahd was at home waiting for Bria to come over. He had something he needed to get off his chest and it couldn't wait. He'd taken the liberty of having his top chef from Parle's come over to make them dinner.

The sensuous aroma of the delicious food Freud made for them had Gahd's mouth watering; he just needed Bria to get his dick hard to seal the night. He stood in the mirror adjusting the tie he wore, making sure his lavender shirt was fully tucked in his navy-blue pants. Tonight's theme was "grown and sexy," and he couldn't wait to get to the sexy part.

The doorbell chimed and suddenly, he was nervous. He was about to tell her something that he'd never told any woman before and he was afraid. Gahd turned on his Okera personality and opened the door.

"Hey baby, damn… come in," he said dumbfounded by Bria's look. She was sporting a tiny black swing dress that stopped mid-thigh with a plunging neckline. Her heels looked to be a little over four inches and were sexy.

"You look good," Bria said shyly as she rubbed her hand down Okera's muscular chest while biting down on her bottom lip.

"Thank you, baby, dinner is ready and is right this way," Okera said as he held his arm out to guide her to the dining area. The room was dark with only candles and a couple recessed lights over the table lighting the room. It was beyond romantic and Bria loved it.

"A strawberry and pecan spinach salad to start you off… You have crushed strawberry and mint leaf ice water. The entrée will be served in fifteen minutes," Freud said before exiting the room.

"You are such a sweetheart; you're so romantic, baby," Bria said with a grin.

"I had to… I—I love you Xiibria. I'm in love with you and I want this relationship more than anything. This is all new for me, so

I'll make mistakes, but if you're patient with me, I promise I'll do everything in my power to make you happy," Okera confessed. He was only glad Koki wasn't around to clown him for sounding like a bitch.

"I'm so glad you do, because I love you too, O. After everything I've been through, I never thought I'd fall in love again, but you changed that for me. You've brought me nothing but sheer happiness since we've been together, and I don't ever wanna be without you," Bria admitted. She didn't care about his ex-bitches or his past; she only wanted to focus on the right now.

O pulled Bria onto his lap and the two of them kissed passionately until he picked her up and laid her on the table. He pushed up her dress and ripped off her panties before pushing her flexible legs up by her head. With a lick of his lips, Okera slid his chair up to the table and feasted on Bria's juicy pussy. His fingers toyed with her g-spot while his tongue licked her like a lollipop.

"The entre—" Freud started before he quickly turned around and hurried out of the room. His face was bright red as he stood smiling at what he'd just saw before him.

"I guess I missed that selection on the menu," Freud said aloud and returned to the kitchen.

∼

Carti sat with his head resting on his hands as he thought about his next moves. He was awaiting Bryce's arrival; they needed to have an important meeting. A few minutes later, Bryce arrived with a smug look on his face as if he was without a care in the world.

"Wassup Carti, how can I help you sir?' Bryce asked.

"I want you to do what the fuck I'm paying you to do. Why the hell am I being followed out here in these streets by the pussy ass pigs!" Carti spat with venom.

"What are you talking about? No one's following you, I made sure of it. I haven't heard anything about you being a person of interest, unless..." Bryce started before his voice trailed off.

"I told you the FED's were trying to build a R.I.C.O. If that's true, there's nothing I can do about that. It's out of my division and I don't even have any connects in there to look out for you," Bryce admitted.

"What the fuck you mean, there's nothing you can do about it? You better find some friends in the Fed's real fucking quick or they're going to find a dead pig soon," Carti said with grit as he eyed Bryce with a murderous glare.

"I'm going to need more money if I have to do all that!" Bryce shouted as he stood to his feet.

Carti picked up the backpack from the floor next to his desk and grabbed a stack of hundreds then threw it at Bryce's face.

"Take this and get your dirty pig ass out my face before I make some bacon," Carti shouted.

Bryce quickly picked up the money and stormed out of Carti's house. His slipped into his car and sped off without hesitation. He didn't even notice Bria parked behind him as he rushed off. She sat in shock as she watched her partner leave this huge house with a stack of money tucked under his arm. It was exactly what she needed to see to move on with her investigation of Bryce.

"I knew his ass was up to something. Dirty ass nigga!" Bria said aloud before she pulled off.

∼

"Listen up everyone, today, we're going to pick up our person of interest for the "Limb Murders" as well as the murder of Boo. This isn't just a regular suspect. Word is he's some sort of drug lord turned mogul. Of course, he's not the person who carried out the crimes, but we do believe he may have orchestrated them or knows who did. He's not considered armed and dangerous because he doesn't have a record, but we do believe he has security that trails his every move and they are armed and dangerous," Dobbs said with a stern look before continuing with the briefing.

"Damn, this muthafucka sounds like mufuckin' Nino Brown or some shit," Bria whispered causing Bryce, Curt and Reed to erupt with laughter.

Thug Alibi

"This is no laughing matter. You assholes fuck this up and it'll be your asses being laughed at," Dobbs spat with his finger pointing at the group, commanding respect.

"Here are a few pictures of our suspect; we'll also hand out some sheets to carry in the car with you."

Bria's laugh quickly faded as her eyes focused on the photo of the man on the projected screen. It was the love of her life, her boo, her lover. She felt sick as she listened to Dobbs identify him by name.

"This is Okera "Gahd" Ali. He is a heavy hitter in these streets and he is not one to be fucked with. His name carries weight like the military. He is not a suspect, but a person of interest. Sams and Jones, I'm putting you two on this to lead the recovery team. Remember, don't push too hard; we want him to feel comfortable talking to us. Alright, be safe out there. Happy hunting," Dobbs said before dismissing the team.

Bria hurried out and to the restroom to throw up. She couldn't believe the man she'd fallen in love with could possibly be behind those heinous murders. She just wanted to get to the bottom of it all, before she judged him off some bullshit lie.

When Bria finally came out, Bryce was standing there smiling from ear to ear. He couldn't wait to lock up her man; it was almost as if he knew she and Okera were together.

"Come on B, let's go get this muthafucka," Bryce said leading the way. She trailed behind him slowly and her stomach turned the closer they got to his house. She walked with Bryce up to the door as the police held their warrant up in the guards' faces. Bria stood in front of the door as Bryce pressed the bell on the side of the door.

Okera pulled open the door with a smile the moment he saw Bria. Bryce pushed open the door and his smile faded. He was no longer Okera; he was now Gahd. His jaw was clenched tight as Bria stood there unable to speak or move. She watched as they walked him down to the squad car without cuffing him. He looked back at her then smiled; he knew she was shocked. But it was only the beginning of surprises for her.

She decided to ride shotgun; there was no way she could drive.

She sat in the car with O while Bryce talked to a few of the other officers outside.

"You're so beautiful when you're in shock. Don't worry baby, I got you…" Okera whispered. Bria turned and held his hand with a smile before Bryce got in. She was going to fix this shit, if it was the last thing she did.

To be continued…
Thug Alibi

Subscribe

Text Shan to 22828 to stay up to date with new releases, sneak peeks, contest, and more....

Want to be a part of Shan Presents?

To submit your manuscript to Shan Presents, please send the first three chapters and synopsis to submissions@shanpresents.com

CPSIA information can be obtained
at www.ICGtesting.com
Printed in the USA
LVHW04s1930180918
590557LV00017B/300/P